MW00943118

Eyewitness Report

- A Novel -

Marilynn J. Harris

Cottage Publishing

Cottage Publishing
Boise, Idaho
www.marilynnjharris.com

First published by Cottage Publishing: 2/22/2019

ISBN- 13:9781799075783

Printed in the United States of America

For information or to order more books please visit our website:
www.marilynnjharris.com

Or Contact:
Cottage Publishing
8530 W Targee Street
Boise, ID 83709

Books by Marilynn J. Harris

The Moon Mountain Series

On Top of Moon Mountain: book one

Beyond the Idaho Mountains: book two

Return to Terror Mountain: book three

The Enigma Series

Enigma Fire: book one

Enigma Winds: book two

Enigma Sun: book three

The Magic Christmas Kite

Song of the River

Freedom is never more than one generation away from extinction. We didn't pass it to our children in the bloodstream. It must be fought for, protected, and handed on for them to do the same, or one day we will spend our sunset years telling our children and our children's children what it was once like in the United States when men were free.

Ronald Reagan

Table of Contents

One

Mrs. Ingrid Westerly

My name is Daniel Levi Jacobson. When I was born, I lived in a big old white house on the corner of Idaho and Twenty-third Street, in downtown Boise, Idaho. It was an older, established neighborhood, in fact, the house that we lived in was the same house that my dad had grown up in. When my parents got married, they purchased the house from my grandparents, for only a few hundred dollars.

Like most of the children in my neighborhood, I stayed in my same family home until I was old enough to move out on my own. People were more settled in those days, they rarely moved around. No one was rich or poor. We had just enough. We had food, our family, a roof over our heads and friends. That's all we needed. Of course, almost everybody in the neighborhood knew each other, because we had been neighbors most of our lives.

In the summertime each child played outside from daylight until sunset, stopping only for lunch or to snack on a cool dripping popsicle or an ice cream cup that you ate with a flat round wooden spoon. Most days you could see the neighborhood kids running through the lawn sprinkler, just to cool off. Then it was back to playing again.

Every morning the entire neighborhood would come alive with chaotic squeals and laughter as the children gobbled down their breakfast and rushed outside for the day.

The youngest girls played hopscotch or jump rope on the sidewalk. Others dressed up in dress up clothes and high heels, and took their baby dolls for a walk in their doll strollers.

The grade school boys played marbles, or raced up and down the alley on their prized shiny bicycles. Every one of the boys used cards from a deck of cards, and attached the cards to the wheel brace on their bike with a clothes pin. Each bicycle clattered in rhythm as the tires spun around, and popped when the spokes of the bicycle passed by the attached cards. Of course, at nine years old, I thought my 26" opalescent red Schwinn that I got for my birthday was the fastest bike on the block.

The teenage girls would sit on the front steps of one of the houses, and quietly laugh and whisper secrets to each other. They would giggle with joy when one of the boys their age sat down beside them on the step to flirt for a few minutes.

The girls never seemed to tire of watching the older boys play kick the can up and down the middle of the street. The game paused only when an infrequent car approached.

There was a small city park right across the street from our house and on many hot summer days all of the kids from blocks around would head over to the park to play. No adults ever went to the park with us, there was no reason for them to go. We would play games like red light, green light, freeze tag, Red-Rover, and mother may I.

My favorite game of all was ollie-ollie over. One of the players would shout ollie-ollie over and then toss a tennis ball over the roof of the restroom building. The building was just big enough that you could not see the people on the other side. At the start of each game we would choose an equal number of kids for each team. Both sides had older and younger kids alike.

You would toss the ball over the building. If someone caught the ball on the other side as it rolled off the roof, they would run around the building and drag one person back with them to their side. If no one caught the ball they would pick it up, and shout ollie-ollie over and then throw it back over the roof. The side with the most players at the end of the game was the winner. The younger children loved playing at the park because the older kids often allowed them to play group games with them.

There was a tall metal slide that stood directly in the center of the park. Each young child knew that they were finally getting big when they could climb the tall steps alone and slide down the slide by themselves. In the middle of the summer the silver metal slide was too hot to even touch, let alone slide down, but in the Fall, it was amazing. It was high, steep and slick. You slid down so fast that you would fly off the end of the slide and land sitting on your bottom on the ground. We all loved it!

Each Halloween we dressed in homemade costumes and set out trick or treating long before the sun ever went down. We thought nothing of going to every house in the surrounding neighborhood. None of the parents went with us. They all stayed home to hand out candy.

We ran from house to house as fast as our legs would run. Filling up our entire pillow case bags with a variety of tidbits before returning home late in the evening, totally exhausted. We got treats like apples, cookies, homemade popcorn balls, raisins, and of course our favorite store-bought small candy bars. Parents never seemed to worry about unwrapped or homemade goodies when I was young. It was just your typical carefree neighborhood of the mid 1950's.

They did not have public kindergarten in those day, but many of the neighbor kids went to Mrs. Conrad's kindergarten class with me at the Christian Church downtown. On my first day of school, my kindergarten teacher Mrs. Conrad told the class, "If you listen, you will learn." So, I always listened, and she was right because learning came effortlessly for me. Throughout my school years I over achieved, always following the rules and doing the right thing.

When I started grade school, I attended the small neighborhood school three blocks from my house. I walked to school by myself every day from the first grade through the sixth. All of us walked everywhere alone. We knew the neighbors, and we felt safe.

As I grew older, I walked to Junior High and High School each morning with the rest of the neighborhood brood. It wasn't until the beginning of my senior year that my best friend Bill got a job after school and he bought a car. It was a 1956 Ford Victoria. I rode to school with him for the rest of the school year. Our lives were innocent, content and secure. Life was much simpler then.

My dad once told me a story about my grandfather, his father. He said that one summer when my grandpa was only thirteen years old, he rode his bicycle all the way to Jackson Hole, Wyoming from Boise. He packed some food and water and took off with his German Shepherd dog to go and visit some relatives.

That was an amazing story to me, because the roads were not well maintained and it had to have taken him several days just to get there. My dad said that my grandpa slept by himself on the side of the road, with just a blanket and his dog. The safety of the trip alone would be unheard of in today's world, but he did it.

I was the youngest in my family. My mom said, "I was her surprise blessing." I came along ten years after my sister, Rebecca. I didn't mind being younger than Rebecca, because Rebecca was my idol. From the day I was born she was my second mother. She held me on her lap all of the time, and carried me everywhere until I was almost three years old. Rebecca continually told everyone that I was born, just for her.

When you are the youngest of six children you learn something from each of your siblings. I learned good manners from Rebecca, and my oldest brother Mark taught me how to talk. My sister Rose taught me how to walk, and my brother John taught me how to write my name and all of my letters. Out of all of the life lessons that I learned from my siblings, I think the most important lesson that I ever learned was from my brother Matthew. Matthew was kind, thoughtful and well-liked, and he taught me to be honest, truthful, and trustworthy.

As I grew up, I never forgot the valuable lessons that I learned from each of my siblings. I never wanted to disappoint them or let any of them down.

All of my brothers and sisters were very loving to me. When you are the baby of the family you feel really special, but within a few short years one-by-one you are forced to say goodbye as your siblings grow up and leave you at home all alone. Rebecca and Rose got married, Matthew left for college, and Mark and John joined the army. I thought my heart would break every time one of my brothers or sisters moved on with their lives. Soon, I was the only sibling left in our big old white house, and I hated it.

After all of my siblings moved away, I often played by myself. I would sit for hours and write stories about things that I had seen or heard about. I would fill up every page in a note book. My mom would buy me another note pad, and I would soon fill it up too. I had stacks of handwritten stories piled in one corner of my closet.

Television was a new invention that came to the Boise Valley around 1953. By 1957, almost every household had some sort of watching device. Our television was small, but I found it fascinating. To think that someone could talk in a completely different location many miles away, and I could watch them on our small television set, seemed absolutely amazing to me. I was intrigued, so I spent at least an hour each afternoon watching the television.

My mom worked part time for a lady downtown, and my dad worked for a meat packing plant, about six blocks down the street from our house. They were both gone most of the day, and if I didn't talk to my friends in the neighborhood, I rarely talked to anyone.

The upstairs of the house was empty after each of my brothers and sisters moved away, so my parents moved my bedroom downstairs near them. They cleaned out a large storage area on the east side of the house, and turned the room into a wonderful big bedroom just for me.

I got my brother Matthew's old bed, and my brother John's desk. The ceilings in my room were high, and the wooden floor creaked when I walked around, but I loved my new room. My bedroom was on the main floor facing east towards the next-door neighbor's big picture window.

The new bedroom was huge, and I was so glad to be downstairs closer to my parents. I had to admit, it was a little scary staying upstairs all alone after my brothers and sisters left. For much of the day I just hung out alone in my bedroom, so I was excited to move downstairs where I felt more included.

Our house was only about ten feet away from the house next door. My new bedroom window looked directly into the neighbor's large picture window. I could see everything that went on inside of their house.

The neighbors next door were Dwayne and Ingrid Westerly. Mr. and Mrs. Westerly had lived next door to us ever since I could remember, but I had never really seen them until I moved into my new room. All I knew was that Mr. Westerly worked in the lumber yard on the other side of town, and Mrs. Westerly stayed at home most of the day and cleaned house and occasionally worked in the yard.

They were very private people, they seemed to just keep to themselves. Mr. Westerly was gone most of the time, leaving his wife alone at the house from early morning until late in the evening.

My mother once told me that Dwayne Westerly had met Mrs. Westerly when he was in the army, stationed in Germany. After the war he married her and brought her to America.

Ingrid Westerly cleaned her house continually. Her large picture window gleamed. She washed her windows at least once a week, and as I looked out through my bedroom window, I could see that her entire house was immaculate inside. She kept very busy cleaning her house, but for some reason she seemed really lonely. The Westerly's had no children, and I never saw anyone visit her house. She was very thin, but she was a beautiful lady with fair skin and extremely long silky light-brown hair. She never went anywhere, even Mr. Westerly rarely took her with him when he left. Day after day she just stayed in her house all alone.

One day Mrs. Westerly looked over at me while she was washing her windows. I smiled and waved hello, and she timidly smiled back at me, and slightly waved. Our houses were so close together we could almost touch fingers if we opened up the windows. From that day forward, we always waved to each other, as if we were old friends.

It was comforting to me to have an adult close by, I didn't feel so abandoned. Just knowing there was someone around, gave me peace of mind.

I had been downstairs in my bedroom for several weeks, and I was feeling really comfortable. It was the beginning of June, and school was out for the summer. The weather was starting to warm up, and in warm weather our whole family liked to sleep with the windows open at night to let the cool night air flow through. Very few houses had air conditioning in those days, and the fresh outside air always helped us to fall asleep faster.

After turning off my light, I crawled into bed, and suddenly I heard shouting coming from next door at the Westerly's house. The shouting got louder and louder, so I left the lights off, and crept over to the window to see what was going on. They had two small windows on both sides of their large picture window that they too had opened up, so I could hear every word that was being said at their house.

I silently watched as Dwayne Westerly shouted and screamed at my timid new friend. She was pleading with him to stop, but he continued to scream louder. I watched in horror as he slapped her across the face and threw her to the ground. He was shouting at her and calling her names. His shouting was so clear, I felt like I was inside their front room with them, and he was also shouting at me. He was slurring his words, like he had been drinking. He was so angry that he was completely out of control.

It really scared me. I felt sick. It was the first time that I had ever seen anyone beat someone up before. I fell to my knees and covered my ears to get the screaming to stop. I didn't know what to do, because I was only nine and a half years old. How could I possibly stop a huge six-foot tall man from beating his wife. All I could do was sit on the floor, in front of my window covering my ears as tight as I could, wanting the shouting, crying and screaming to go away.

Finally, the turbulence stopped, and I snuck back up to the window to look out. All of the lights were on inside of their house, so I could easily see in. The house was now quiet, and I could not see Mrs. Westerly, but I could clearly see Mr. Westerly and he was passed out on the couch, on the far side of the room.

Sadly, I climbed back into bed and tried to sleep. I felt like crying, I was so upset. I wanted to go tell my parents what I had seen, but I just couldn't move. The horrible images of that poor woman being beaten, would not go out of my mind. I kept picturing Mrs. Westerly the way that she had looked over the past few weeks when she innocently smiled and waved at me through the window. She was so thin, and frail. I thought to myself, "What could she have done to make him so angry at her?" I stared at the ceiling until I finally fell asleep.

The next day as I was sitting out on the front steps of my house, I saw Mrs. Westerly walk out of her front door. I was delighted to see her up and walking around, but she never even looked up at me. She had her head completely covered with a scarf, and even with the weather getting so warm she had on a heavy coat with the collar pulled up around her neck.

Slowly the delicate neighbor lady walked down the street, probably going to the corner grocery store. She kept her head down towards the ground, and she walked really slow, and kind of crippled along. Although, the Westerly's had lived next door to me all of my life, until I moved downstairs across from them, I had never even noticed them before. I felt bad for her. She was my friend. I wondered if she would ever smile and wave to me again.

I didn't tell my parents about what I had seen at the westerly's the night before, but I did get out my tablet and pencil, and I wrote down everything that I could remember. I was afraid that my parents would move my bedroom back upstairs if they found out about the problem at the neighbors, and once again I would be upstairs all alone. So, I decided not to tell them anything about what I had seen.

My parents never argued, and all of this was new to me. My whole family was polite and considerate towards each other. I was raised in a very proper family. Of course, I was so much younger than my siblings that they never had anything to be angry with me about. Our entire family was honest and trustworthy. We had high morals, and we were taught to tell the truth no matter what. That's why it was so difficult for me to not tell my parents about the Westerly's and their fighting.

After that first evening, there was shouting and hollering every night. Mr. Westerly came home drunk and screamed at his wife, slapped her around and broke things. This was just the normal way of life for them. He shouted the same things at his wife night after night, and every morning I would wake up and write down everything that he had said. My parents always told me that I had a photographic memory and perhaps that is true, because I found it relatively easy to quote every word that Mr. Westerly would shout.

Every day I would watch Ingrid Westerly through the window as she would sadly clean up the destruction that he had left behind from the night before. She never smiled or waved at me again. Even as she washed her windows, she never even looked my way.

From my bedroom window I could see her blacken eyes, and she held one arm in a towel sling. No one else knew about her situation, because no one ever saw her except for me. If she went outside, she covered her head with a scarf, and hid her injuries and bruises, so that no one would know.

The rest of the time she stayed securely hidden inside the prison walls of her house; faithfully waiting for her husband to get home from work. Knowing that he would be drunk, and the brutality would start all over again.

It was confusing to me, but it seemed that it was all that she knew. She had nothing else. I was nine years old, and the next school year I would be in the fifth grade. Although, I was still in grade school, even I knew that their situation was not right. No one should be allowed to hit someone else, but I didn't know what I could do to help Mrs. Westerly.

Each night I would lay in my bed praying that the screaming would stop. My window was closed, but with their two side windows open, I could still hear him shouting. I tried not to look out of the window at night anymore. It upset me too badly, besides there was nothing I could do but lay in my bed tightly covering my ears. Eventually, the shouting would stop, and I could go to sleep.

My sister Rebecca lived in a small apartment on the south side of town. She was married and she was going to have a baby in a few months. Out of all of my brothers and sisters, Rebecca was the one that I missed the most. She was always the person I could talk to and trust. It was going to be a good day because my mother had left me some change to catch the city bus so I could go across town, and spend the day with Rebecca.

The bus stop was only a block from our house, and I could catch it there and ride the bus across town, all the way to my sister's. I could hardly wait to see her. I hadn't seen her since I had moved my bedroom downstairs.

Rebecca fixed us grilled cheese sandwiches, tomato soup and chocolate milk for lunch. We talked and laughed, I hadn't felt this good in weeks. I finally decided to tell my sister about the Westerly's and how scared I had been with their fighting.

My sister told me, "I remember hearing them fight late at night after you had gone up to bed." She looked at the ground and continued, "Danny, you know Mrs. Westerly was pregnant four different times and each time she lost the babies." Then my sister looked me directly in the eyes and said, "I always felt sorry for her, because her family was so far away. She has no friends, and she seems really young. I don't think that Mrs. Westerly is that much older than I am. In fact, she is probably around Mark's age." My sister then shook her head and replied, "I never saw her husband hit her, I just knew that he yelled a lot, but she did seem very frightened and alone. Mom tried to be friends with her, but Mr. Westerly didn't want his wife to talk to anyone."

"I tried to be her friend too," I told Rebecca. "I smiled and waved at her every time I saw her in the window, and at first she smiled and waved back, but now she never even looks up at me." I questioned, "Why does she let him hit her? Why doesn't she run away?"

I confided in Rebecca, "Mr. Westerly is so angry with her, and he always shouts the same accusations at her night after night. I know because I have written them down." He says, "You are so worthless. All you do is stay in the house all day and do nothing, while I work my fingers to the bones. That's why I have to stop at the bar, and have a few drinks with my friends each night. I need to relax and unwind and forget."

I told my sister, "Then he starts throwing things, and hitting her and screaming. Mrs. Westerly cries and pleads with him, but he acts like he can't even hear her." Then he screams, "I never should have married you. I wanted to marry Ellie, she was the love of my life. When I went off to war; she wrote me a letter, and broke off our engagement." He whines and screams as he talks and then he says, "When she wrote me, she told me she was marrying my cousin, Harvey. I was heart-broken. Then I got you pregnant, and I felt I should marry you and bring you home with me." He continues to whine and he mutters, "Many of the guys just left their pregnant girlfriends there in Germany to have the babies on their own, but I did the proper thing and made you one of the war brides, and brought you back with me."

He continues to bawl and scream as he says, "Oh, I tried to do the right thing, so I married you and brought you here to Idaho. We hadn't been in Idaho three weeks when you lost the baby, and I wished I had never brought you here." He sobs and begins to wail, "Oh, I miss Ellie more and more every day. Every time I see her, it starts all over again. Ellie and my cousin Harvey have four kids and I'm stuck with you, and I have none. I wanted a son, that's all I ask...just one son to carry on my name."

Mr. Westerly keeps talking, and he gets quieter and quieter, but I can still understand him. Right before he passes out each night, he says in a whiny voice...Harvey and Ellie have two sons, and I have none."

My sister looked at me and said, "Danny, Mrs. Westerly was only a seventeen- year-old girl when Mr. Westerly brought her to America. She came all the way from Germany, and she has nowhere else to go."

That night after visiting with my sister all day I felt more compassion towards Ingrid Westerly than I had ever felt before, so I stood in the darkness keeping watch over her house. I opened up my window again to help cool off my room. Everything seemed different now, I knew what to expect, the shouting would not alarm me like it did in the beginning, and I sensed more of an odd closeness with Ingrid Westerly after talking with my sister. I felt like I should stand guard. She needed someone to be with her, although, there was nothing I could do to help her, or to stop him from hurting her. I realized that Mrs. Westerly really was a kind lady, and she was trapped with no way to escape. The least I could do is stay with her, so she wasn't all alone.

As I watched out my window, I saw Mrs. Westerly stand and peer out into the darkness for a few seconds, looking over my way. At first, I thought she might have been looking at me, but the room was so dark behind me, I didn't think she could even see in. The lights were on inside of her house, so of course, I could clearly see her front room.

Late that evening Mr. Westerly finally arrived home. It was considerably later than he usually got home, and he seemed much drunker. He could barely walk, but he started right away throwing things around. He was like a wild animal, stumbling from one thing to the next destroying everything he touched. Glass was breaking, and a giant antique lamp shattered as he threw it across a table, and then I saw him tear the pictures off the wall and throw them in the middle of the room. He ripped down the drapes and then started breaking the windows; he was completely out of his mind this time.

I was getting scared and tried to walk away from the window like I usually did at night, but I couldn't pull myself away. I stood in the darkness and just stared at the drama taking place in front of my eyes. Mr. Westerly was totally irrational. It was terrifying. I thought maybe I should go and call the police, but I didn't want to make things worse for Mrs. Westerly.

It was strange because even Ingrid Westerly was acting different than I had ever seen her act before. She didn't seem frightened of him this time. She calmly just stood in the center of her front room watching this crazy man destroy her house. She didn't plead with him or beg like she usually did. She patiently just watched as he went from one item to another throwing everything into a heap in the middle of the room.

Suddenly, he stopped dead in his tracks; he finally noticed that his wife was acting differently. She didn't seem afraid of him anymore. Something had changed, and she was no longer terrified of him like she had always been. She had had enough. Apparently, Mrs. Westerly decided that she would never let him hurt her again. While standing only a few feet away from the deranged mad-man that she called her husband, she raised the pistol that she held securely in her hand and emptied three shells from the gun-barrel into the evil-looking crazed person in front of her. He wobbled towards her pleading for a second chance, but it was too late. She had been waiting for him, and this time she was glad that he had come home. She shot him with one of his own guns.

As Dwayne Westerly lay dead on the floor I watched Ingrid Westerly walk over to the phone, and dial the police to tell them what she had done. When she was finished, she put down the phone and walked slowly over towards the broken picture window; she looked directly at me standing in the dark shadows of my bedroom, staring out at her in total disbelief.

I was shaking so violently I couldn't move away from the window, and I could hardly breathe, but I saw her calmly smile and slightly wave at me. She then turned around and walked over and sat down in a chair to wait for the police.

I was in shock. I was in grade school at Madison Elementary and I had just witnessed my neighbor lady shoot her husband.

Within a few minutes I heard police sirens blaring down the street. They were coming to arrest Mrs. Ingrid Westerly. I quickly ran to the front room to tell my parents about the police sirens, and they automatically followed me out to the front yard to see what was going on.

The entire neighborhood lit up with flashing lights from all of the police cars. The lights were bouncing off of the surrounding houses as they whirled around in slow motion. Neighbors exited from every front door, until the streets were swarming with families clad in pajamas, bathrobes and slippers. Many of the younger children were already asleep, but they were quickly awakened by the numerous loud police sirens, and the ambulance.

Our tranquil neighborhood came alive with unanswered questions and babble. People came from blocks away to see what had brought so much attention to the Westerly household.

Families were in disbelief to find that the quiet, frail German lady, Mrs. Ingrid Westerly had killed her hard-working husband in cold blood. As the neighbors chattered, I realize that no one truly knew this couple… only me. Most of the neighbors had never even talked to Mrs. Westerly in the eight and half years that she had lived there.

I had never actually talked with her either, but we had a special friendship that didn't need words. I could see and hear her miserable life's story played out in front of me every night, through her large picture window. I heard the screaming, and I watched him beat her.

Most of my life, I had been told that I behaved much older than the other kids my age. It might have been from being raised by all adults, because my siblings were so much older than me. I was a deep thinker, and I always wanted everything to be proper and just. My world was black and white, so even at nine and a half years old I felt a deep sadness for this abused lady that had been brought here from half way around the world.

Our family was not a stranger to guns. We lived in Idaho, and my father had taken each one of us deer and bird hunting every season. In fact, we had several rifles and hand guns on the gun rack that hung in my parent's bed room. I was a good shot, and I had learned to shoot when I was only five years old. So, watching someone shoot a gun was probably not as traumatic to me as it might have been for someone who had never hunted. I was more concerned for Mrs. Westerly, because she could see no other way out of her abuse.

Later that night, as I sat alone in my bedroom, I wrote down every detail that I could remember from the night's events. I didn't want to forget any of the specifics that had taken place, in case someone questioned me about the situation. I wanted to remember only the truth, and I feared that by morning my thoughts might not be as clear. I wrote down twenty-two pages of notes, starting from the time I got home from my sister's house until I came back to my room after the police had taken Mrs. Westerly away.

Early the next morning, there were news people and cameras lining up and down the street in front of the Westerly's house. The police had arrested Mrs. Westerly for the murder of her husband. The newspaper and television people were asking questions to each of the neighbors, but no one knew anything.

I silently watched as neighbor after neighbor was interviewed and said nothing to help poor Mrs. Westerly. The interviewers ask about the damaged furniture, and destroyed windows, but again, no one had answers.

Finally, I said, "Excuse me sir, my name is Daniel Levi Jacobson, and my house is right next door to the Westerly's house. I was a friend of Mrs. Westerly." At first the camera people did not want to even talk to me, because I was a young child, but they soon realized that I was the only person that knew anything at all about the couple that lived next door to my house.

I talked very precise and mature for my age, and I always told the truth, because being honest is just part of who I am. After I talked with them for only a few minutes the news people realized that I wasn't your normal fourth grade child.

They turned off the cameras and began to ask me questions. The lead news reporter then shook my hand, and introduced himself and said, "Nice to meet you Mr. Daniel Levi Jacobson, my name is James Grattan from KBCI news. What did you need to tell us about?"

I told them word for word what Mr. Dwayne Westerly screamed at his wife each night. I let them know that he came home drunk night after night, and broke everything in his way, and then beat up his wife. I told them how I would cover my ears and try to fall asleep each night.

They listened to me intently and after several questions, they ask if they could see my bedroom. I had told them it was directly across from the Westerly's big picture window where he had been shot.

I took them in the house and let them see for themselves how closely I had been standing as Mr. Westerly broke the windows and tore the pictures off of the wall. Once again, I stood by the open window to show the exact spot where I had been watching as Ingrid Westerly shot and killed her husband.

The newsmen could clearly hear the investigators that were talking next door inside the Westerly's house. The investigators were looking over the crime scene to see if they could make any sense of what had happened at the house the night before.

We could understand every word that the investigators were saying, even as quietly as they were talking, because the ceilings in most of the old houses were high, and the rooms were not carpeted, they had wood floors. All of the sound echoed when someone talked as if they were speaking into a microphone. That's why it was so easy to hear conversations that went on between the houses. Plus, the fact that the two houses were only separated by a few feet of open area.

After an hour or so, the news people left and I sat all alone in my room staring at the giant broken window next door. I would miss my friend, Ingrid Westerly, but at least Mr. Westerly can never hurt her again.

As I sat in my room, I thought about the news people and all the questions that they had ask me. I was absolutely in awe of the television newsmen. Like me they were only searching for the true facts, and I admired that because I believed in truth and honesty.

I spent the next few hours pretending that I was the television news reporter, and I was busy searching for the answers so that everyone would know exactly what had happened at this crime scene. I wrote down notes, and several questions that the reporters had ask me.

Around three in the afternoon, I was surprised because both of my parents came home early. My mom sat down on the couch next to me and said, "Danny, we got a call from the police department this morning, and they want to come over to the house, and interview you because of the shooting that occurred next door. You don't know anything about what happened last night do you?" She looked at me really concerned and stated, "You never even met Dwayne Westerly, did you?"

Because I was always so incredibly honest, I quickly looked down at the floor trying to decide what to answer; then I told my mother, "Well, I never really met him, but I did hear him yelling at his wife after I moved my bedroom downstairs, across from their large picture window." I gently nodded my head up and down and stated, "I did hear Mr. Westerly shout and scream at her every night. I saw him break things, and then he would beat her up. Mom, he was mean, and I think he hated his wife." My mother was obviously very shaken as I told her, "I couldn't help but feel sorry for Mrs. Westerly, she was so far away from her family. Mom, I tried not to judge them or get involved, but he would beat her, and she had no way to defend herself, and she couldn't stop him."

My mother looked at me in shock before saying, "Why didn't you tell us. Where you in danger?"

"Well, I was afraid you would move my bedroom back upstairs where I would be all alone again," I timidly told her.

"Oh Danny," my mom said as she hugged me tight, and wiped the tears from her eyes. "This whole thing is so crazy. I am so sorry. My poor baby. You must have been so scared all the time."

My dad sat on the other side of me shaking his head. Then he put his arm around my shoulders and said, "Oh Danny, we forget that you are only nine and a half years old, you act so much older than your age. I am so sorry, we had no idea all of this was going on. You know, to tell you the truth, I personally had never even talked to Mr. or Mrs. Westerly before. In all of the years that they have lived next door I have rarely even seen them."

Suddenly, the doorbell rang. It was three policemen, and the news reporter and camera man that had been there earlier in the day.

Once again, I repeated the same things that I had told the reporters earlier. Then I went to my room and got my stacks of notes that I had written over the past few weeks.

My mother spoke up in my defense and she told them, "If Danny says Mr. Westerly shouted at his wife and beat her, you can trust that to be true. Although, he is young, he thinks and talks much older than other children his age."

The main newsman smiled at me, and patted me on the leg. He said, "Yes, we interviewed all of the neighbors up and down the street, and although they didn't know anything about Ingrid and Dwayne Westerly, they all spoke very highly of Daniel."

He smiled at me again before saying, "We weren't sure if we should trust such a young witness, because this is a murder case. The investigators interviewed all of the neighbors, and every one of the neighbors stated the same thing, "If Danny Jacobson told you what he saw through the window, you can believe it to be the truth, because Daniel never lies."

He added, "Daniel, we know that you are on summer vacation, but we also contacted the Principal and a couple of the teachers from your grade school and they too spoke very highly of you." He smiled as he replied, "Daniel Levi Jacobson you are a very respected young man."

That night my parents and I watched James Grattan as he shared the story about the murder of Mr. Dwayne Westerly on the six o'clock news. Mr. Grattan did a wonderful news report. He quoted some of the statements that I had shared with him from my notepads. He also stated, "Mrs. Ingrid Westerly has been arrested for killing her husband." In conclusion he said, "The murder is still under investigation."

I just stared at the television in disbelief. I was intrigued by the complicated workings of the television station. Mr. Grattan spoke honest and precise and he looked exactly as he did when he was at my house doing the interview with me. I could tell that he fully believed in honesty and always letting the public know the truth.

We visited with the news people and the police investigators on six different occasions following the murder. Within a few days they had collected all the information from the neighbors and me that they needed, and we didn't hear from the police or the news people again for over six months.

Then on one blustery day, a week before Thanksgiving the news station called, and asked if they could meet with me and my parents on Saturday afternoon at 1:00 p.m.

The news cameras were soon set up for a personal interview, along with James Grattan, and the three policemen that had interviewed me before. After everything was set in place a black sedan pulled up in front of our house. The cameras were all pointed towards me as a lady slowly got out of the backseat of the car. Although, I had never actually met her face to face, I knew right away who the lady was. I beamed with delight as Mrs. Ingrid Westerly emerged from the sedan, and ran towards me and bent down and wrapped her arms around my shoulders, and hugged me and kissed my cheeks.

Through her tears and broken English, she told me, "I am free because of you, my young friend. The judge has granted me self-defense, and they are allowing me to go home, back to Frankfurt, Germany. I am leaving on the train in two hours, and I will travel all the way across America to New York City, and then I will sail across the ocean to Hamburg, Germany, back to my family." As Mrs. Westerly hugged my face and cried, she uttered, "Oh young Daniel I can never thank you enough for being in the window next door. You heard my cries for help, and they told me you wrote everything down on tablets."

My mother directed Mrs. Westerly to come sit on the couch and I sat beside her. She then continued, "When the doctors at the prison checked me out, and requested x-rays, they discovered I had six broken ribs that had healed and been rebroken. They could tell that both of my arms had been broken several different times, and just left to mend on their own. Eight of my fingers had been dislocated and were severely damaged from being bent completely backwards on several different occasions.

My jaw had been fractured and I had three broken teeth towards the back of my mouth. My husband also crushed the toes on both of my feet, by stomping on them with the heel of his boot on various occasions."

She went on, "Mr. Westerly was a big man and he often beat me until I passed out. After meeting with countless doctors, each one noted numerous scars and fresh bruises to show that my abuse was ongoing. Proving that everything that I told them about my life with my husband was true."

She continued, "They also, interviewed my husband's boss and other people that he had worked with. They were told that he often came to work drunk, he hollered a lot, and he had a really bad temper."

She said, "I was told that the people that he worked with had been told that he always regretted marrying me. They said he complained about me all of the time, but they stated that none of them had ever met me."

She paused before going on, "Because of your extensive written testimony, they accepted the fact that my husband was the person that broke out the windows, destroyed the pictures, and all of the furniture and tore down the drapes. You had written in your notebooks the exact same statements that I had told them."

She told me, "Apparently, we had both stated that we had never actually talked to each other. Yet, we told the authorities the same things. The judge said that proved how out of control Mr. Westerly truly was."

Mrs. Westerly held my hands between her hands and looked directly into my eyes as she told me, "Young Daniel that last morning was the worst. My husband told me before he left for work that he hated me, and that he planned to come home that evening and burn down the house and everything that was in it… including me. I had nowhere to go, and I knew of no one that could help me. I was scared to death, I honestly didn't know what to do. So, I was there waiting for him with one of his own guns, just in case he really did try to burn the house down."

She took a deep breath and looked down at our hands before telling me, "Although, I had never shot a gun before I waited until he was really close to me, and I pulled the trigger three times. I knew that his guns were always loaded. He constantly said there was no reason to have guns in the house if they were not ready to use."

She sighed before going on, "When he first came home, I watched him and I could tell that he was going to do exactly what he had said he would do. He was destroying everything that he touched, and then piled it in the center of the room. That is why the judge ruled his murder self-defense, because they could tell that my husband had planned to kill me first."

She went on, "You know Daniel, I hardly even knew my husband when I married him. I had only seen him two times when I became pregnant, and he told me he would marry me and bring me to America." She covered her face with her hands, and as she wiped the tears from her eyes and said, "I was just a young girl, I never wanted to leave my family or my country, but I did what was right, and what was expected of me."

I just stared at the beautiful German lady before me. Her hair was even longer than I had remembered. It was thick and flowing softly across her shoulders and down her back. Also, she had put on some weight since I had seen her last, and she looked much healthier and her entire attitude was joyful and happy-go-lucky. She seemed like a totally different person than the timid lady that I first saw in the window. She had beautiful laughing eyes that kind of squinted when she talked. Mrs. Westerly was so delicate and graceful, and I was amazed at how intelligent she was.

Ingrid Westerly talked to me like we were old friends; she had so much to tell me. I was thoroughly engrossed in everything that she was saying to me. I just smiled, laughed and nodded my head up and down. I was stunned by the things she was saying.

She continued, "Because of your accurate notes they talked with Ellie and Harvey Westerly, my husband's cousin and his wife." She hugged me once again and stated, "Because of you young Daniel, and all of your precise writings, they verified everything to be true. They compared what I told them with what you had written in your notes, and we both told the exact same statements. Now I can go home. Thank you, thank you thank you my dear young friend from the window."

As we visited for a few more minutes my mother got out a piece of paper for me to write down my name and address. I handed it to Mrs. Westerly, so she could write to our family from Germany when she gets home. Both my mother and my father hugged Mrs. Ingrid Westerly before we said our final farewells.

Before getting back into the car Mrs. Westerly paused for a moment. She took one last look at the house next door that she had been held captive in for the past several years. The house was now empty inside, and the windows had all been boarded up. Relatives of Dwayne Westerly had come and sorted through things, and they sold everything that had not been broken or destroyed. They knew that Ingrid Westerly would never be returning to the house again. In the nine or ten years that Mrs. Westerly had been married to her husband, she had rarely seen Dwayne Westerly's family. He had been estranged from his family long before Mrs. Westerly ever came to Idaho. So, she had only met them one time.

All that Ingrid Westerly owned was the few clothes that had been sent to her at the prison. She had nothing else. She sadly looked at the house and shook her head back and forth, and climbed in the back seat of the sedan, and waved goodbye to me as she drove away.

I stood in the front doorway of our house, and quickly wiped wispy tears from my eyes, as I watched her ride off down the street, heading for her beloved homeland. The two of us would forever have a special bond, that started with one apprehensive smile, and a slight wave through the window.

I walked back to the front room as the news people were finishing up. I quietly sat down in the corner chair mulling over everything that had been said in the last hour. My brain was on overload, and I thought to myself as I grinned, "She did know that I was in the window keeping watch over her, and she knew that she was not all alone." I chuckled out loud, "I may not be very strong, but with my tablet and pencil in hand…I am powerful and I can change the world.

Early the next morning, Mom and Dad woke me up to show me that my picture was on the front page of the newspaper. The picture was a wonderful close-up of Mrs. Ingrid Westerly hugging me after she had been released from prison. The caption stated that the murder case was ruled as self-defense because of the written eyewitness report of the Westerly's young next-door neighbor, Daniel Levi Jacobson. It said that Mrs. Westerly had struggled with extreme abuse from her husband for many years. The article said that she would be returning to her homeland of Frankfurt, Germany

By New Year's Day, we received our first of many letters from my pen pal in Germany. We were pleased to hear that Mrs. Ingrid Westerly had finally returned home safely after all of her terrifying years in America.

Our family received letters from Germany at least three times each year. When I was eleven years old, we received word that Ingrid Westerly had married again and was living happily just a few miles down the road from her parents.

On my thirteen birthday I got a special birthday card from Germany stating that Mrs. Westerly had just delivered her first baby with her new husband. A healthy baby boy, she named him Daniel Levi.

I never saw her again, but my dear friend Ingrid, and I remained pen pals for over 40 years. One afternoon I received a letter from her son

Daniel, he wrote to tell me that his mother, the lady that I knew as Mrs. Ingrid Westerly, had died in her sleep.

Two

The Boise Bomb shelter

Before my tenth birthday, I started submitting stories to magazines and I entered several writer's contests. Each day after finishing my schoolwork I would write. To be good writer, you also need to be an avid reader, and I was. I have always been very disciplined, so it was my homework first, then I would allow myself to write. I became absolutely obsessed with reading and writing.

By the time I was in the eighth grade at North Junior High, I was in a special honors English class. While in that class, I won a National writer's contest where I competed against over 10,000 other students throughout the United States. All of the participants in the contest were between the ages of twelve to eighteen-years-old. I was one of the youngest writers in the contest. Because I won that competition, I was personally chosen to attend and write about a very special event for Idaho, the opening ceremony for the new Boise Bomb Shelter.

For me to be invited to this ceremony was an enormous privilege, because the dedication of the new Bomb Shelter was one of the biggest events that Boise, Idaho had ever observed. I was grateful to all of my teachers. They had been the ones who had chosen me to go as a representative for the Boise School System, and to write about this special event for the Idaho newspaper. It was a huge responsibility for someone my age. I knew that I would be one of the youngest students in the valley to attend the private ceremony, and I was absolutely overwhelmed to be trusted with such an honor.

The new Bomb Shelter was to be developed because of a letter that was sent to the American people. On September 15, 1961 a personal letter from President John F. Kennedy was sent to all of the people of the United States. He wrote, "My fellow Americans, nuclear weapons and the possibility of a nuclear war are facts of life that we cannot ignore today."

President Kennedy explained, "The federal government will soon begin a program to improve the protection afforded you and your communities through civil defense."

The new Civil Defense program was an agency of the United States Department of Defense. It was actually, the Cold War Home Front Civil Defense System, and it was to take effect immediately. Civil Defense drills were enacted throughout the nation. Non-military efforts were used to prepare the American people in case there was ever an attack on our own U.S. soil.

Civil Defense is a volunteer-based emergency response organization. It operates at a National level under the Department of Defense. Their main purpose was for communication to quickly alert the general public to impending danger. If our country came under attack the Civil Defense authorities notified the local authorities, and the information was delivered through the local authorities and channeled down until it had reached every individual person. A plan of action was set up through all schools, businesses, arenas, theaters, and homes. There was also, radio contact for people riding on trains, planes, buses or automobiles. Fallout shelters were rapidly being developed and thousands of emergency pamphlets were being handed out throughout the nation.

This was a terrifying time in our country's history. The entire nation lived in fear of a nuclear war. Parents oftentimes felt helpless when it came to protecting their children. In the beginning they were hesitant to even send their children to school for fear they wouldn't be close enough to shield them if an attack occurred. It was clear to every American that if the federal government was this fearful; no one was safe.

All schools were training their staff members on what to do in case of nuclear attack. Every staff member had a certain job to do to help get the students to safety in the event of an attack. The schools practiced emergency evacuation drills on a regular basis.

Most school cafeterias were set up as a combined cafeteria and bomb shelter. They were also used as a cold storage space to store food, an extra workroom, and a theatrical production hall. Using the basements as dual-purpose areas helped keep the cost down when creating all of the bomb shelters.

The first choice that was printed in the information pamphlet was to send each child home with their parents if there was enough time to prepare before an attack. Most people in authority felt there would never be enough time to get the students home safely. So, evacuating the students out of their classrooms, and keeping them secured in the basement bomb shelter was the second and most likely choice.

A National survey was developed, one that would identify all public buildings with fallout shelter potential. They were to be marked accordingly. The Federal government was devising a way for fifty million Americans to survive a nuclear war by rushing to the nearest fallout shelter.

Each large city had sirens that did drills that sounded precisely at noon once a week. A steady blast for 3 to 5 minutes meant take cover at once; it signaled it was not just a drill. They had to make the sirens very distinct, especially in areas that had tornadoes sirens and hurricane warnings. The air-raid sirens were placed in all major cities, and the fallout bomb shelter signs were quickly created. The sign was a metal square sign with a large black circle in the center with three yellow triangles placed inside the circle. They were solidly made so that they could last for many generations and not fade or corrode. People got so they could easily recognize the sign whenever they were in the area of a bomb shelter.

The signs were developed by Robert W. Blakeley of the Corp of Engineers. He made them so that they could be seen on dark streets. In those days, almost every adult smoked, and they were created so that the signs could be easily read by the light of a cigarette lighter.

The 3M corporation (best known for making scotch tape and post it notes) manufactured over 400,000 shelter signs for which the government paid less than a penny a piece. The signs popped up everywhere. In New York alone the Army Corps of Engineers contracted with 38 architectural firms to inspect 105,244 large buildings. Eventually, some 19,000 would become shelters.

Many large firms spent a lot of money to make their bomb shelters very posh. The Chase Manhattan Bank spent $49,000 on "compressed" wheat biscuits in banana and chocolate flavors to stock their five-story shelter.

Most of the shelters just had low ceilinged basements equipped with the barest necessities like bedding, medical supplies, wheat crackers, and government provided toilet paper. They had to get some sort of toilet facilities themselves, and they were hard to come by. Many of them created a commode by cutting out the seat of a chair and placing a pail under it. Each bomb shelter was equipped with food for two weeks, first-aid kits, safe water, a generator and blankets.

The Boise Bomb shelter was constructed in 1961 during the Cold War, a time when there was rampant fear of a nuclear attack by our Soviet enemies. Around that time the United States government decided to place intercontinental ballistic missiles in the Mountain Home Military Base, only fifty miles from Boise. It was later unearthed in some of the Soviet documents that Boise was a potential target if the nukes ever started flying. That was the reason the Boise Bomb Shelter was established.

The citizens of the Highlands area of Boise formed The Highlands Community Shelter Inc. The organization was formed so they could get a community bomb shelter built in their neighborhood. It was to be the first of its kind in the nation. The 'Highlands Community Fallout Shelter' was the first prototype community fallout shelter in the United States and it was dedicated for use as a center of recreation, business and youth activities. It was also ready to meet the requirements of Civil Defense research and a National emergency of any scope.

The facility at 600 W. Curling Dr. Boise, Idaho was designed by a Boise architect by the name of Edgar B. Jensen and constructed by the Welsh Brothers Construction of Boise. The community fallout shelter cost $122,000 to complete. The funding for the project came from the Federal Civil Defense Agency and from the sale of stock which was $100.00 per share for the families in the Highlands.

The Bomb Shelter was an underground concrete building designed to house multiple families for an extended period of time in the event of a nuclear attack. The structure was two stories high and 14,000 square feet of steel reinforced beams, and it includes a diesel generator, kitchen and family dormitories and decontamination showers. The Boise Bomb Shelter was located in the Highlands subdivision about 16 miles from Bogus Basin Ski Resort. The community shelter was built in the side of the mountain with a large double door to the entrance, and a large double door at the back exit. The structure was covered with dirt from the nearby hillside. The building had a laundry room, a loud speaker system, record player equipment and the latest fresh air filtration system.

Because this was the first Bomb Shelter of its kind in the United States, the opening ceremony was one of the most exciting events to ever occur in the state of Idaho. Many important people came from around the nation to witness this unique event.

Some of the prominent people who attended the ceremonies were: Idaho Governor Robert E. Smylie, Col. James Keel the State Civil Defense Director, Norman Jones of Ada County, the Boise City Civil Defense Director and members of the Board of the Highlands Community Shelter Inc. Also, attending was the Boise Chamber of Commerce, Clyde Friend the Director of the Spokane Civil Defense Department, The Ada County Commissioners, Boise Mayor Robert L. Day and members of the Boise City Council.

Many other influential people from around the country were invited to the opening ceremonies. They came for the opportunity to witness first-hand the development of the nation's first prototype fallout shelter. They studied the plans, the extensive architecture, and they listened to the speakers tell of the need and extreme purpose for building a shelter such as this. Because this was the first shelter of its kind in the nation, they came with hopes of someday building a shelter of this type in their own communities.

Although, the shelter was successfully completed there was a lot of resentment throughout the Boise Valley when the shelter was finally dedicated. Many people who didn't live in the Highlands area felt angry that the Bomb shelter was built for Highlands residents only, because the shelter was designed to save only 1,000 people.

The shelter was created for members only, and the Highland board committee threatened the public to stay away. They chose 35 to 40 security guards from their own membership to stand guard to keep the rest of the community out.

Around that time, the government had discussed building massive concrete shelters all around the nation, much like the Boise Bomb shelter. Shelters that they knew could withstand an explosion, but they decided they would be extremely costly. So, they opted for the next best thing; shelters that would shield citizens from radioactive particles that would likely be blowing around in the air for weeks after the attack.

The government officials soon decided that the fallout shelters would do nothing to safeguard people from an actual bomb, but the new shelters would give them some form of protection. Several basements in the larger buildings in downtown Boise were also set up as shelters. The Hotel Boise, the Capitol building and most of the hospitals were a few of the buildings that had been designated as fallout shelters. They were concrete, well-protected and set up with rations, blankets, fresh water and restroom supplies.

Writing about the Boise Bomb Shelter for the Idaho newspaper was a tremendous accomplishment for my future writing career. Throughout the following months and into the next few years I wrote numerous articles for the newspaper. Several of the articles had to do with other Civil Defense Bomb Shelters located around America.

As I followed up on the bomb shelter program, I discovered that many of the shelters throughout the country never even received their supplies. The initial panic of a nuclear war started to fade with time, and people started to complain about everything pertaining to the bomb shelters.

The New York Times told of a Harlem woman who told reporters, "Who would ever go down there to those filthy cellars anyway? The rats are as big as dogs." She stated, "If fallout came, I'd just run."

A second story was published on the front page of the Washington Post bemoaning the fact that most of the designated shelters would be little more than 'cold, unpleasant cellar space, with bad ventilation and even worse sanitation."

The locations were a bigger problem, because two-thirds of the fallout shelters in the United States were in 'risk areas.' Neighborhoods were so close to the strike targets that they would likely never survive an attack in the first place. In New York, for example most of the government shelters could be found in Manhattan and Brooklyn. Despite the fact that a twenty-magnitude hydrogen bomb detonated over midtown would leave a crater 20 stories deep and drive a firestorm all the way to the center of Long Island. It was stated in Life Magazine, that even that far away, occupants of a fallout shelter might be barbequed, but the feds always thought that an atomic war would be waged with only military installations as targets.

The Washington Post wrote only a few weeks after the shelter program had gotten started that, "The public's feeling about the Civil Defense program was one of helplessness."

By January 1962 Life Magazine encapsulated the sentiments of the general public stating, "An attack wouldn't be just one bomb, but it would be many bombs at once and everyone in the shelters would be killed."

By 1971 the government decided to phase out all of the stock piles of rations in the shelters. Eventually, many building owners donated their shelter rations to charities which shipped them to Africa and Bangladesh. In New York some of the biscuits would end up with farmers to be fed to their pigs.

Many felt that the hundreds of fallout shelter signs were just ominous symbols stating, "This signifies the end."

On September 15, 1972 the property where The Boise Bomb Shelter was located was purchased by the Independent School District of Boise City. The School District used the facility for the administration offices and a storage of school records, furniture, and film reels etc.

Three

The First Frozen Man

By the time I was nineteen years old, I had published over 600 articles in newspapers, magazines and periodicals. Because I started my writing career at such a young age, I began signing my work as D.L. Jacobson, instead of Daniel. My family said it made me sound older and more distinguished, so throughout my entire seventy-year career, I have always been known as D. L. Jacobson.

At twenty years old I did freelance writing for three major marketing companies, and around that time I started accepting some of the overseas project-based assignments. By the time I was twenty-one I had visited the United Kingdom, Sweden and Germany. While in Germany I thought about going to see my pen pal Ingrid Westerly, but my time was limited and I was forced to put our visit off for another trip. Sadly, that time never came.

I also, did a unique article on The Who's New Year's Eve concert called 'Psychedelic Amani' that took place in The Roundhouse in London, England. Also performing that night were the groups The Move and Pink

Floyd. I thoroughly enjoyed the music concert assignments because I was granted private interviews backstage with all of the musicians.

Probably the most notable music interview that I have ever done in my career was with the popular rock group, The Beatles. I did a private interview at the EMI's Abbey Road Studio in London. They were just starting their new album called Sgt. Pepper's Lonely Hearts Club Band. All of the band members were kept under constant guard at that time because John Lennon had bragged to a reporter that "The Beatles' were more popular than Jesus." That angered a lot of people so the group was held under heavy guard everywhere they went. That's why they felt it would be more convenient if I came to the studio for the interview.

They had nearly lost their lives in the Philippines a few months earlier after offending dictator Ferdinand Marcos. Individually, they were all very nice people, and the interview went well, but the band was becoming quite arrogant because of their popularity throughout the world. They complained that they were tired of touring and facing all of the frenzied fans, so they had taken a break for a few months. I met up with them shortly after they started touring again.

As a freelance writer I was at liberty to work on several projects at one time. I did all my writing on a project paid basis, so it was actually better for me to be working on several different assignments at the same time.

***

One of the most exciting and unusual endeavors that I have ever worked on is when I went to Glendale, California to learn about cryonic suspension, or the freezing of Dr. James Hiram Bedford. Dr. Bedford was a seventy-three-year-old retired American psychology professor at the University of California. He had written several books on occupational counseling.

Dr. Bedford had a boundless desire for adventure. In 1958, nine years before his death he went on an African Safari, a wilderness tour of the Amazon rain forests, and extensive travels to Greece, Turkey, Spain, England, Scotland, Germany and Switzerland. He was also one of the first to drive the Alcan Highway to the Canadian Northwest and Alaska.

Many believe that is why he chose to take an even more fearless and uncertain journey by being frozen. He was dying of kidney cancer, and it had metastasized to his lungs. Dr. Bedford felt that they would find a cure for cancer within a few years, and he wanted to be frozen until a cure was found.

Cryonics is a Greek word that means cold. In June 1965 the Extension Society was so anxious to complete their project that they even offered to try to freeze someone for free. There had already been a tragic near miss on May 20, 1965 when they tried to freeze Wilma Jean McLaughlin of Springfield, Ohio. She had suffered from heart and circulatory problems. She almost became the first person frozen for a possible reanimation in the future, but she died ahead of schedule, and the attempt to freeze her was abandoned.

The husband was all for freezing, but the rest of the relatives and their minister were against it. The physicians would not aid in the experiment either. The hospital administrators and trustees met in an emergency meeting and refused to go along with certain procedures after death. Besides the "capsule" or insulated container was not available yet, because she had died too soon and they were not prepared.

Another tragic near miss occurred a year later. Dandridge M. Cole a brilliant scientist and technological engineer was deeply impressed by all of the private literature that he had read on suspended animation.

He had even expressed a wish to be frozen after death to several of his friends and colleagues. Cole was only 44 years old when on October 30, 1965 he suffered a fatal heart attack. Although, his friends knew of his wishes, his family wouldn't go along with the idea, so his wishes were ignored.

A success of some sort finally occurred on April 22, 1966. An unidentified woman around 66 years old who had been privately embalmed, was straight frozen. The freezing was done by Cryo-care Corporation in Phoenix, Arizona. She had come all the way from Los Angeles, California.

It was one step forward towards bringing an extended life to others via cryogenics. They feared her memory which is a matter of fine molecular placement would disintegrate because there was too much time between death and freezing. So, within a few months the woman was removed from suspension.

Finally, the freezing of Dr. James Bedford took place on January 12, 1967, in Glendale, California a suburb of Los Angeles.

Lynden B. Johnson was President of the United States. The Vietnam War was in full swing, and the Beatles were the top performing group of the nation. The political and social focus was on the "Great Society" which meant the notion that poverty and social ills could be overcome by government programs. This was the beginning of massive changes in the way the American people thought. Science was very trendy in 1967.

Because so many doctors and hospitals were against Cryonics, the doctors who were working with Dr. Bedford knew they needed to choose a hospital that would follow through with the process. It was stated that Dr. James Bedford was a quiet, honest and a very responsible man. A man who often pondered the purpose of life, and the meaning of death. He was married, and he was a World War I veteran. Dr. Bedford had some good friends that ran a Seventh Day Adventist Hospital and Nursing Home that were willing to help in the procedure.

Dr. James Bedford was to be the first cryonic suspension. His body was frozen with dry ice to minus 79 degrees centigrade and would be stored in liquid nitrogen at minus 196 degrees centigrade. It was said that he had patches of ice pieces still placed on top of his body when he was put into an insulated box, and he was still wrapped in the bed sheet. He was then covered with one-inch thick slabs of ice.

Dr. Bedford remained frozen because his wife and son followed through with his process to make sure nothing went wrong. They kept him guarded so that he would not be allowed to thaw out and decompose.

Dr. James Bedford was reported to have been perfused with cryoprotective agents whereas the other person, the unidentified woman was embalmed. Dr. Able, the attending physician at the time of Dr. Bedford's death said that he applied artificial respiration and external heart massage to maintain circulation of oxygenated blood while the body was being cooled. He packed ice all around Dr. Bedford on the hospital bed then they waited for Robert F. Nelson, the President of the Cryonics Society of California to arrive.

Two hours after being frozen the body was transferred to an insulated box, still wrapped in the bed sheet and covered with a thick sheet of dry ice.

Dr. Bedford was transferred out of the hospital by relatives six days later. Then he was moved in the back of car a by Robert Prehoda. Robert Prehoda was affiliated with the newly formed Cryonics Society of California.

Robert Prehoda soaped up all of the windows in the back of his car so that no one could see in through the windows. He drove his station wagon home and parked it in the garage. Everything was fine until his wife discovered that he had a frozen body in the back of their car. Reports stated that she became hysterical, and she made him take it away.

He drove it up on a hilltop, away from their house. The next day he transported the frozen body to the Ed Hope Cryo-care storage center in Phoenix, Arizona. There the frozen body would be placed in a liquid nitrogen environment for his journey through time.

Because the freezing of Dr. James Bedford was so intriguing to me, I actually followed his progress for many years after he was first frozen. I went back to check on him on May 25, 1991. At that time, he had been frozen for over 25 years. The pieces of ice that had been left on his body when he was transferred in 1967, were still there.

The last time I checked on Dr. Bedford he was being held at the Alcor Life Extension Foundation in Scottsdale, Arizona. It is a non-profit organization that uses cryonics in an effort to save lives by using cold temperatures to preserve someone for decades until a future medical technology can restore that person to full health.

Even after writing about Dr. Bedford on several different occasions, Cryonics is still very confusing to me. The last time I checked on the doctor he had been frozen for over 50 years. Caretakers have moved him from one location to another, continually keeping watch over his frozen body.

The unsophisticated world that he knew when he was first frozen has radically changed since his death. Every person that first helped him when he began this secretive voyage, is now deceased. His entire family and every friend that he has ever known is gone. If he were to awaken from his frozen sleep today, he would be completely alone.

This was such an unusual article for me to write about. It made me realize how impetuously our world was advancing. There were so many transformations taking place in science, in medicine, in churches, and in our cultural. People's beliefs in life and death were totally different from the beliefs of their ancestors.

Our world was rapidly altering into a world that many of us could no longer recognize. With every editorial that I published I learned about things that I would never have imagined as I was growing up.

As I completed this article I couldn't help wondering if Dr. Bedford would now have different thoughts about being the first person ever frozen. I am quite sure that he had no idea that he would spend generation after generation in his cryonic state; and after 50 years of remaining frozen, medical science had still not found a cure for his cancer.

Four

Walking on the Moon And Woodstock

The year 1969 was a year of many diverse happenings. At 9:32 on July 16, 1969 Apollo 11 took off from Kennedy Space Center with three astronauts aboard: Neil Armstrong, 'Buzz' Aldrin and Michael Collins. They traveled 240,000 miles in 76 hours, to walk on the moon.

At 10:56 p.m. EDT on July 20, 1969 Neil Armstrong and Buzz Aldrin separated from Apollo 11 leaving Michael Collins on board alone, and they landed on the moon in a lunar module, Eagle. Armstrong immediately radioed to mission control in Houston, Texas and he spoke to more than a billion people listening back home and he said, "The Eagle has landed." Then he stated, "That's one small step for man, and one giant step for mankind."

Armstrong was the first human to walk on the moon. At 11:11 p.m. Buzz Aldrin also walked beside him on the moon. Together they took photographs, planted an American flag, collected some of the surface dust and then spoke to President Richard Nixon.

They placed a plaque on the surface of the moon that read, "Here men from the planet earth first set foot on the moon July 1969 A.D. We came in peace for all mankind."

The men were told not to say or do anything religious because NASA did not want them to offend any of the people listening over the radio. But Buzz Aldrin quietly produced a small flask of wine and a piece of dry bread and he softly read from the Gospel of John. He couldn't resist being the only Christian to ever receive communion on the moon.

When the men were finished with everything they needed to do, they returned to the lunar module and closed the hatch. They discovered that a switch to a crucial circuit breaker had broken and they notified NASA to try to fix it from earth. The men then tried to relax, and they slept the rest of the night on the moon, inside the lunar module. The next morning Aldrin jammed his pen into the mechanism creating a makeshift switch.

At 5:35 p.m. Armstrong and Aldrin successfully docked and rejoined Michael Collins on Apollo 11. At 12:56 a.m. on July 22 Apollo 11 began its journey home. The three astronauts successfully landed in the Pacific Ocean at 12:51 p.m. July 23, 1969.

One of the things that they discovered after studying the accumulated moon dust was that it had a strange pungent smell. Armstrong stated that the dust smelled a lot like wet ashes from a fireplace.

Another interesting fact revealed after they returned to earth was that the three astronauts could not afford life insurance for their families before they left for the moon, because they were such high risk. So, they came up with an ingenious plan; they got together before they left and made several hundred autographs and left the autographs with a trusted friend. In case they did not return from the moon, they knew that the autographs would be valuable and could be sold to support their families.

Another interesting fact that most people did not know is that the astronaut's spacesuits were created by several little old ladies in a small sewing shop.

Another small detail that is rarely mentioned, is that the flag that they planted on the moon surface was blown away by the rocket blast when the astronauts returned to earth.

***

On August 15, 1969, just 23 days after the astronauts returned to earth, I attended the Woodstock Music and Art Festival in Bethel, White Lake, New York. It was absolutely amazing how totally different the Woodstock assignment was compared to that of the Moon Walk from only a month earlier.

My journalism career was thriving and I couldn't be happier. I loved my life. I spent hours and hours every week flying from one location to another, eating in restaurants and living in expensive hotels. I was in my early twenties at the time, and I was living the life that every young writer could only dream about.

Around that time, I began to notice a massive transformation in the beliefs of many of the college students that I interviewed. I realized that they significantly changed their views of life from high school to college graduation. By the time they graduated from college they had slowly turned towards socialism. It had actually started in the early sixties under President Jimmy Carter. At that time things were beginning to rapidly shift and after students went to college many of the graduates had out-grown the old-fashioned traditions of their parents.

The hippie generation had started in America a few years earlier, and that was the beginning of a strange new carefree era for the American youth. It began on the college campuses in the United States and then it spread to other countries, and into Canada and Britain. It was a countercultural movement that rejected the mainstream American way of life.

Of course, Woodstock, was an entirely different kind of assignment for me than normal. I had to dress totally opposite from how I usually dressed.

I often did such high-profile interviews that my normal way of dressing was very professional and up to date. I donned the Ralph Lauren Look from Bloomingdales. I wore white flannel suits with big lapels and heavily pleated, deep cuffed, corduroy pants, and I was obsessive about wearing well-made shoes. I had my Italia men's brogue oxfords shined and polished each morning as I passed by the airport shoe shine booth. I felt I needed to dress so that people would know that I took my work seriously.

I knew that going to Woodstock would be different, so for Woodstock I bought some baggy worn-out bell-bottom pants; some big sun glasses, a tie-dyed saggy t-shirt, some sandals, and a thin bandana type scarf that fastened around my head. I had been growing my hair a little longer for the past few weeks and when I got to the festival, I looked just like everybody else, so no one even noticed me. For the first time in years I was dressed like everyone else my age.

Unlike the other five hundred thousand young adults that were there, I was not quite as awe-struck as so many others seemed to be. I was there to write an article describing the event, and they had come to be transformed and enlightened.

There were young people there from every walk of life and every income bracket. Several of the concert-goers even brought their children. They had come to Woodstock for many different reasons; adventure, curiosity or maybe finding a place to belong.

Woodstock was not the first of its kind, but it was the biggest event of its kind. When the event was first being planned the organizers were told that they were to have several police units to control the event, but when the day arrived for Woodstock to begin the police were told not to go.

Many of the concert goers had drugs hidden in their clothes, inside their cars, in their shoes, or in their underwear, but it didn't matter because no one ever searched them. Every kind of drug was readily available. There were dealers roaming freely throughout the crowds. There were others who stayed back in the woods and everyone referred to them as "High Street."

Most of the young people were stoned 100% of the time. I saw a guy selling acid like he was selling hot dogs at a hot dog stand. I felt kind of sorry for some of the younger people, because you could tell that this was the first-time, they had used drugs. They just kind of sat on the ground, in the cold sloppy mud, and stared straight ahead.

I noticed one young girl, about sixteen years old, who sat in the same spot for over seven hours. I left and when I came back by, she was still sitting there, she had never moved. I wondered what she would tell people back home about Woodstock. Would she tell them what a wonderful experience it was, or would she say that she just sat in the cold icy mud, stoned out of her mind for three days?

No one seemed to have a care in the world. Everyone you passed seemed friendly and relaxed. It truly was three days of peace, tranquility, music and drugs. I am quite sure that if not for all of the free-flowing drugs there would have been a lot more trouble amongst the concert goers. There had been brutal fights, arguing and several arrests at all of the other concerts of this type.

Many of the attendees that I talked with had plans to meet up with other people when they arrived at Woodstock. But the crowds were so massive once they got there that they could never find the people they had planned to meet. Sadly, it was often their friends who were supposed to bring the food or the tent. It didn't seem to matter to anyone when they couldn't find who they were looking for, they would just hang out with someone new. Someone they had just met…no one cared.

One girl told me that all that she brought with her to eat was a bag of carrots, so she shared them with everyone around her. If you saw someone drinking a soda, and asked them for a sip, they just gave it to you. People would go to sleep under their tent and wake up in the morning with dozens of new people sleeping beside them. Again, no one cared.

It was amazing to watch how everyone could peacefully co-exist and bond for the entire weekend despite the rain, mud, cold, lack of food and limited facilities. Cleanliness was never an issue, and by the second day most of them just went to the bathroom on the ground.

Woodstock would be a total turning point for the younger generation. They always felt that they were a minority, but at Woodstock they discovered they were the majority and there would be no stopping them. They soon discovered that when they united that many young people together…they had power. They figured out that together they could change the world. For three entire days they were under no authority. The world as we had known it would never be the same after Woodstock.

The music, the sharing and the collective independence were life-changing. They became aware that anything was possible. They realized that they embraced taking chances and following their own dreams. Their ideals of what was important in life, and what they wanted to let go of manifested in the three days at Woodstock.

The youth of Woodstock were committed to living by their own principles, they believed in universal human rights, infiltrated creative expression, the loving care of our planet, and the power of one to make a difference.

The festival was opened by guru Sri Swami Satchidananda. He said, "I have recently talked to the Grandson of Mahatma Gandhi. He asked me what America is up to, and I told him that you are into helping everybody. He told me it was time to also help with the world's spirituality."

He told the crowd, "I am overwhelmed that all of the youth of America is here to learn of fine arts and music. Music controls the whole universe. Sound energy, and sound power is much greater than any other power in the world. We have gathered here to make some sounds, to find peace and joy through celestial music." He said, "The entire world will watch and they can see what America's youth can do to all humanity."

Because I have never used drugs, I was on the outside watching the activities of the rest of the concert goers. I constantly walked through the crowds and observed everything that was going on. I was not self-absorbed like most of the attendees appeared to be, and I thoroughly enjoyed all of the bands and the music.

The guru was correct about one thing, Woodstock was a groundbreaking beginning for many of the performers. Their live performances at Woodstock moved them up in popularity for countless generations to come. Many of the new, unknown performers became household names after Woodstock. Woodstock would be known as the iconic moment in music history.

Two things that the hippie generation did not like was war and doing anything for profit. They were not aware of it, but the men who organized Woodstock planned to make a lot of money on the concerts. At first the organizers could not find any place that would even let them have such an event. No one wanted thousands of unwashed, doped-up ruffians destroying their property.

Finally, a dairy farmer with 600 hundred acres decided he would lease them his land for $75, 000. He was told that there would only be around 50,000 young people at the event. The organizers then scrambled to get big names that would come. The three top names were Janis Joplin, The Grateful Dead and The Who.

As the word got out more and more concert goers decided to come to Woodstock. They just piled into someone's Volkswagen and came with no thought of food, water or a change of clothes. Before the event started the tickets were sold for $18.00 per person for all three days.

The organizers had planned to sell tickets at the gate for $24.00 a person for those who did not sign up in advance. When it was time for the event to begin, they discovered there were no fences or gates around the property, everything had been knocked down, so whoever came late, got in free.

The traffic was so congested on the road to the concert, that many of them just left their cars twenty miles on down the road and walked in. The stalled traffic was so bad they had to bring the performers in by helicopter because no one could get through.

Although, the organizers had secretly planned on around 250,000 in attendance, there was twice as many concert goers that showed up as they had intended. They had allowed only three toilets for every 10,000 concert goers. When the torrential rain started the out houses overflowed and there was deep sloppy mud, sewage and filth everywhere.

When Woodstock ended the entire valley was over-run with piles of trash, destroyed fields, debris and sewage. There was never any plan for clean-up. Everyone just took off when the concert was done, and left garbage piled everywhere. The concert-goers showed absolutely no respect for the owner of the farm. It would take several years before the land was usable again. The farmer sued the organizers for $35,000 in damages to his property.

Woodstock was a strange reality for me. It was such a disturbing contrast from the innocent, moral, black and white world that I had been raised in back in Idaho. I had always been taught to be considerate of other people, and to treat people the way that I would want them to treat me.

The total disregard for authority was something I had never really witnessed before. The concert goers who attended Woodstock thought only of themselves. At that time in history the youth started reflecting on social experimentation and it soon would become the new norm.

Epic is the word that was oftentimes used to describe Woodstock. Epic music, epic drugs, epic rain, epic peace, epic love...The innocence of the youth of America would never be the same.

It was later reported that there were two deaths on the way home from the concert and over 4,000 were treated for injuries, illness and adverse drug reactions.

Five

Kent State University

On May 4, 1970 members of the Ohio National Guard fired shots into a crowd of Kent State University demonstrators. Killing four and wounding nine students. The event triggered a nationwide student strike that forced hundreds of college and universities to close for a several days.

An aide to President Richard Nixon suggested the shootings had a direct impact on National politics. The shootings showed a deep political and social division that divided the country during the Vietnam War Era.

When Richard Nixon ran for President, he pledged that if he were elected, he would end the war in Vietnam. Things went well for the first few months after he became President. It looked like the war was slowing down. Then on April 30, 1970 President Nixon had American troops invade Cambodia at the headquarters of the Viet Cong, the place the Viet Cong had been using as a sanctuary. This invasion caused a major unrest at many colleges throughout the country, and I was sent to the university to find out first-hand what was going on.

My plane landed in northeastern Ohio early in the morning, on the first of May. I headed out to the University directly from the airport, because I had been told of a rally that was to take place on the commons at Kent State University that afternoon.

Many protests occurred that day, all across the United States, on several different college campuses. Anti-war sentiment was high. At Kent State University an anti-war rally was being held at noon, May 1, 1970, just as I arrived. The commons area is a large grassy area where other rallies and demonstrations had been held.

Fiery speeches against the war were given and a copy of the constitution was burned to symbolize the murder of the constitution because congress had never actually declared war in Vietnam. Yet everyone called it a war, and many soldiers had lost their lives. Another rally was planned for noon on May 4th.

That evening in downtown Kent everything began peacefully with the usual socializing and partying, but events quickly escalated into a violent confrontation between protestors and the local police. The exact cause of the disturbance is still not clear, but bonfires were built in the streets of downtown Kent. Cars were stopped, police cars were hit with bottles, and store windows were broken. The entire Kent police force was called to duty as well as officers from the surrounding communities

The mayor declared a state of emergency. He called the governor and they ordered all bars to be closed. The discussion to close the bars angered the students, and the crowds increased.

Police eventually succeeded in using tear gas to dispense the crowds in downtown areas. Forcing them to move several blocks away, back towards the campus.

The next morning the mayor met with other city officials and a representative of the Ohio Army National Guard. There had been threats made to downtown businesses and to city officials. There were rumors that radical revolutionaries were in Kent to destroy the city and the university.

They feared that the local authorities would be inadequate to take care of the situation. So, they called in the Ohio National Guard. When the guard arrived at Kent State University, they witnessed a terrible scene. The ROTC building, on the campus of the university was on fire. The burning building was next to the commons and there were hundreds of protestors surrounding the building.

When the fire trucks arrived, the protestors jeered and mocked the firefighters. Some even sliced the fire hoses as the fireman tried to put out the burning building. Hundreds of demonstrators cheered as the building burned to the ground.

Confrontation between guardsmen and demonstrators continued into the night. Tear gas filled the campus and numerous arrests were made. By morning on Sunday May 3rd nearly 1,000 Ohio National Guardsman occupied the campus. Making it look like a military war zone. The day was sunny and warm and many of the students even visited with the guardsman.

The governor flew to Kent and he was very upset about what was happening. At a press conference he issued a provocative statement, he said, "The campus protestors are the worst type of people in America." He stated, "Every force of law would be used to deal with them." It was assumed by both the National Guard and the university officials that a state of martial law was declared. In which control of the campus resided with the National Guard rather than the university leaders. All rallies were banned.

By Sunday evening further confrontation between protestors and guardsman occurred, and once again rocks, tear gas and arrests characterized a tense campus.

On the morning of May 4, 1970, the university officials attempted to inform the campus that the rally was prohibited, but still a crowd began to gather. By noon the common area contained approximately 3,000 people.

I estimated that there were approximately 500 core demonstrators gathered around the Unity Bell and another 1,000 were cheering them on. About 1,500 people were just spectators standing around the perimeter of the commons. Across the commons, in front of the burned-out ROTC building stood about 100 Ohio National Guardsmen carrying lethal M-1 military rifles. I stayed far enough away from the crowds to keep out of the way, yet close enough to hear and see everything first hand.

Initially the rally was supposed to be peaceful, but the university still tried to cancel the gathering. The president of the University, Robert White feared the demonstration on May 4th would be dangerous so he distributed 12,000 leaflets stating that the event had been cancelled, but the leaflets were ignored.

Shortly before noon the head of the guard ordered the demonstrators to disperse. Then a police officer riding in a military jeep used a bullhorn so that he could be heard over the crowds. The protestors refused to disperse and began shouting and throwing rocks at the guardsmen.

There were so many demonstrators, that I didn't even know how many of them were students at the University or if they were just anti-war activist from somewhere else. Everything was so confusing it was even hard to tell who was leading the demonstration. There didn't seem to be any one person who was in charge of the group.

Since all of the warnings were ignored the guardsmen loaded and locked their weapons. Tear gas canisters were fired into the crowds around the Unity Bell, and the guard began to march across the commons to disperse the rally.

As the guardsmen approached, the protestors just moved back near the football field. The guardsmen slowly walked towards them as the students backed up the hillside beside the practice field. Soon the guardsmen found themselves trapped because there was a fence around the field and the students were standing all around them on the hill side.

Yelling and rock throwing got out of control and the guardsmen stayed trapped in the field for about ten minutes. Several guardsmen knelt and pointed their guns, but no shots were fired at that time. The guard then began retracing their steps from the practice field back up the hill towards Blanket Hill trying to direct the protestors back to the commons where they had started.

As they arrived at the top of the hill, 28 of the guardsmen turned suddenly and fired their rifles and pistols. Many guardsmen fired into the air or towards the ground. However, a small percentage fired directly into the crowd. Altogether 61 or 67 shots were fired in 13 seconds.

Four Kent State students died. The closest student that was killed was Jeffrey Miller, he was shot in the mouth while standing in the road a distance of about 270 feet from the guard. Allison Krause was in the Prentice Hall parking lot about 330 feet from the guardsmen and was shot in the left side of her body. William Schroeder was 390 feet from the guard and he was shot in the left side of the back. Sandy Schreuer was also about 390 feet from the guard when a bullet pierced the left side of her neck.

Nine other Kent State students were wounded. Most of those students were in the Prentice Hall parking lot, but a few were on the Blanket Hill area.

Joseph Lewis was the student closest to the guard at about 60 feet. He was standing still with his middle finger extended when bullets struck him in the abdomen and left leg.

Thomas Grove was about 65 feet from the guardsmen and was wounded in the left ankle. John Cleary was over 100 feet from the guardsmen when he was hit in the upper chest. Out of all of the students who were shot, but not killed, Dan Kohler was the most seriously wounded.

He was struck in the small of his back from approximately 300 feet away. He was permanently paralyzed from the waist down. Donald McKenzie was the farthest from the guardsmen at a distance of almost 750 feet. He was struck in the neck.

After interviewing several of the students after the shooting occurred, I discovered that many of them didn't believe the soldiers had real bullets in their guns. They thought the National guard was just there to scare them, and to keep order during the rally. That's why they were not intimidated by the guns, and they showed little respect to the guardsmen. They said that the guardsmen had only used tear gas on them before, and that is what they thought they would use on them again.

The University was ordered to close immediately. It was closed down just three hours after the shooting. In fact, hundreds of universities, colleges and even high schools closed throughout the United States. About four million students went on strike.

The May 4, 1970 shootings will be remembered for several different reasons. First the shootings will come to symbolize a great American tragedy which occurred at the height of the Vietnam War era. A time when a nation found itself deeply divided both politically and culturally. It will also be known as the day when the Vietnam War came home to America.

A few days later, shouts of "Burn, Burn, Burn," tumbled through like a Rocky Mountain Spring avalanche. Somehow a lone voice broke through saying, "Let's build, not burn." It had only been 9 months since Woodstock. Thus, was born the idea for Woodstock West. It was an international peaceful response to the violence engulfing campuses from New York to Seattle.

Students pitched tents and built makeshift shelters on a grassy area known as the Carnegie Green. There they debated, sang, talked and tried to make sense of their situation. The spirit of those days repeated the peace and freedom of the namesake of the 1969 music festival, Woodstock.

The guardsmen testified before numerous commissions as well as a Federal court. They said that they fired their weapons because they feared for their lives. They felt the demonstrators were advancing on them and they faced a serious and immediate threat. One of the saddest things that I noticed after the shootings occurred was that most of the soldiers involved in the shootings were about the same age as the college students. Some were even younger than the students they were trying to control.

Classes did not resume again at Kent State University until the late summer, almost four months after the shootings. Faculty members engaged in a wide variety of activities through the mail and off campus meetings that enabled the Kent State students to finish the semester.

Civil suits were filed by the injured students at Kent State and the families of the four dead students. It took several years before an agreement could be reached.

By January 1979 a financial settlement of $750,000 was paid to the wounded students and parents of the students who were killed. This money was paid by the Ohio National Guard.

Months after the shootings occurred many misleading articles were written concerning the National guard and the killings at Kent State University. Several commentaries stated that the students had been shot in the back as they were running away from the guardsmen. This was not true. The journalists who wrote these articles were just trying to once again stir up anger with everyone about the shootings.

This was the first time that I had actually seen false news publication like this. It was difficult for me to even read these made-up editorials because I was there, and I wrote an eyewitness report. It was outrageous to me, because I knew that their articles were fabricated.

The Reverend Billy Graham

The late sixties and early seventies were a time of many changes throughout the world. Martin Luther King Jr, was assassinated on April 4, 1968, and on June 5, 1968 Robert Kennedy was also assassinated.

On December 8, 1968 Nixon declared the Vietnam war was coming to an end. Unfortunately, this did not put an end to the war. It continued on until April 1975.

February 9, 1969 was the first flight of the superpower jumbo jet, the Boeing 747. It could reach speeds of over 600 m.p.h. The demand for air travel had reached high levels. The 747 was six stories tall and weighed 735,000 lbs.

By 1970 the average cost of a house had risen to around $23, 450.00, and rent was as high as $140.00 a month. Gasoline was 36 cents a gallon, and to mail a letter each stamp cost 6 cents. The average household income was $9,400.00 per year. The Dow Jones Individual Average was 838. The voting age had been lowered to eighteen years from twenty-one. Walt Disney World Resort had just opened their new theme park in Orlando, Florida. The beginning of the seventies was an encouraging time in history for most Americans.

In 1971 my own life took on a whole new meaning. I was sent to write an article on the Reverend Billy Graham at a huge crusade in Dallas, Texas. It was an event that would change my life forever.

I had interviewed many celebrities in my lifetime, but this was different. I was in awe of how many people came to the crusade at the Texas Stadium that night. It was a brand-new stadium and the weather was very questionable. It had started to rain and the arena was an open-air stadium, and even with the rain the arena was filled to at least two-thirds full.

When a gospel singer by the name of George Beverly Shea began to sing *"I'd rather have Jesus that silver or gold. I'd rather be His than have riches untold. I'd rather have Jesus than houses or land. Yes, I'd rather be led by his nail pierced hands. Than to be the king of a vast domain and be held in sins dread sway. I'd rather have Jesus than anything this world affords today."* I literally stopped in my tracks. I intently listened to the words that this amazing man was singing. His strong deep voice was absolutely mesmerizing. The lyrics in that song were completely opposite from the rest of the world that I had been writing about over the past few years.

As I listened to Mr. Shea sing, it dawned on me how drastically my life had changed since my youth in Idaho. I now made a lot of money, I traveled all over the globe, and I had met some of the most important people in the world. Many of the things that once bothered me as being offensive, were the things that I had gotten used to and had started to accept as normal. I had discovered that in the business field most people would do anything to be successful at what they do, and I had become one of them.

It occurred to me that I too had begun to believe that money and fame were the most meaningful things in life, just like the people that I socialized with. The words in that song were so simple, and yet they spoke directly to my soul.

This Christian crusade was so unpretentious and innocent compared to the other half of the world that I now lived in. Most people that I associated with were very self-centered. Everything they did was about themselves. Their lives were all about big houses, shiny cars, fancy clothes, being wealthy, and to be more successful than everyone else around them.

By the seventies many people survived on credit cards. If you worked at a job for at least a year, and paid your bills on time, the banks would automatically mail you their credit cards in the mail without you even asking for them. The temptation was too great for a lot of people and they would owe on six or seven credit cards each month.

They would pay the minimum payment on each card, and as long as they paid their minimum payment the banks would slowly increase their credit limit. People began buying more and more stuff; just because they could. People who were once very conservative and cautious with their money, slowly began living on credit. They ate in restaurants a lot more often because they could go out for the evening and enjoy themselves, and not have to pay anything but the minimum required payment at the end of the month. They went shopping because they were stressed, bored or angry, and getting new things made them feel better.

In a short time, they would owe twice as much to each credit card company, as they had income. We soon became a nation of purchase what you want now, and pay for it later.

People would buy new houses, cars, boats and motorcycles as long as the bank told them they could qualify. Families began purchasing whatever they wanted by the amount of the monthly payment, not by the total amount owed. If they could afford a $90.00 a month payment on a new travel trailer, they knew they could have it now, because it fit into their so-called budget. They were not concerned that the total cost would be $18,000. They were only concerned that the bank said they could add on another $90.00 a month, and they knew the bank wouldn't allow it, if they couldn't afford it.

Couples began arguing over money. Many ordinary families would look back and wonder how they ever got in the financial mess they were in. Only the strongest marriages survived.

Most of the people that I interviewed would do anything to be rich and famous. Their lives were hectic, demanding and no matter how hard they tried they could never quite arrive at the top of the success ladder. By the time they reached the top, some newcomer would come along, and instantly replace them. Every month there was a beautiful fresh face on the cover of all of the fashion magazines, someone more handsome and younger; someone more illustrious, wealthier and talented.

Dishonesty was becoming a typical way of life for the majority of prosperous people. Most hard-working Americans would do anything to keep their high paying jobs. Oftentimes they knew that the business practices of their company were not always honest, but they would just look the other way, and do whatever was needed to remain part of the corporate world they had grown accustomed to.

The day of the gentleman hand-shake and trust was almost gone, not with all working-class Americans, but with the "influential" people that I wrote about. That is what I witnessed interview after interview, and I had begun to believe that this was the true way of the world now, but this crusade was different. It was much simpler. I could feel it all the way to my bones, and I once again remembered the Jesus that I had been told about as I was growing up.

Throughout my career I had gained such rapid prosperity that I had shoved my early beliefs to the back burner. Like so many successful people, I felt that I had achieved everything on my own, but when Billy Graham gave his message, I knew he was speaking only to me. I forgot that anyone else was even in the stadium. I was so emotional I wanted to cry like a baby. Soon, I was brought back to my senses when Reverend Graham did an alter call and thousands of people in the audience went forward after he spoke. People came from ever section of the arena.

They even walked down from the very top bleachers, slowly making their way towards the podium to turn their lives over to Jesus. I saw young men and women, old grandpas and grandmas, people from every walk of life and every nationality. There were men in dark suits, and women in short skirts, and even people in their native clothing from different countries from around the world. It was incredible.

People were crying, moaning and raising their hands in the air. They were smiling through their tears and singing "Just as I am" as they slowly moved forward down the aisles. A large number of them were holding the hands of their brothers or sisters, their husbands, wives or neighbors. They were praying and giving praise to the Lord as they walked diligently towards the front of the stadium.

You could tell that people were caught up in their own personal relationship with God, and they were not concerned about what anyone else around them was thinking. They continually walked forward never looking back. You could just feel the powerful presence of the Lord in that place.

I had always believed in God. My family had attended church every Sunday as I was growing up; but sitting in that huge stadium and listening to the Reverend Billy Graham speak was unlike anything I had ever experienced before. I was there to write the true-life story about Billy Graham, but instead I was personally caught up in the overwhelming power of the Christian crusade. When the people around me stood up and started walking towards the alter, I too walked along with them and rededicated my life to the Lord.

I had always been extremely honest, ethical, and trustworthy, and I had lived my life with the highest integrity, but this was different. I knew that I was different. I truly believed that this was the place that the Lord wanted me to be, at this time in my life, and I would never be the same again.

At the conclusion of the service I had the privilege to meet with the Reverend Billy Graham back stage for a personal interview. He was extremely busy, but I was pleased that he would take the time to meet with me for a few minutes.

I was not disappointed, he was so polite, gracious and easy to talk with, and he treated me like I was an old friend that he had known all of his life. He truly was a man of God. I had briefly met other evangelists at other interviews, but Billy Graham was genuinely different.

We talked for a few minutes and then he introduced me to a young lady by the name of Sarah Chandler. She was one of the crusade's personal assistants. Reverend Graham told me, "Sarah knows everything there is to know about the crusades. She will be able to answer any questions that you might have about me, my family, and any of the crusades meetings." As he left, Reverend Graham smiled at Sarah and said, "She has been with the crusade for over three years."

I watched as the Reverend Billy Graham and his team walked away. After everyone was gone, Sarah and I found two chairs over by the wall and sat down. I studied her as we talked. Sarah Chandler was approximately my age, with dark brown hair, dark eyes and glasses. She appeared very professional. She was slender and at least a whole foot shorter than me even in her petite heels. She seemed intelligent and extremely knowledgeable about the crusades.

She wore an attractive navy-blue dress with a delicate pearl necklace around her neck, and two tiny pearl earrings in her ears that matched her necklace.

I noticed that she had a soft but self-assured voice as she told me, "I have been working with the Billy Graham crusade for over three years. I should be able to answer any questions that you might need for your article."

Sarah looked directly into my eyes as she talked to me and I was caught off guard by her self-confidence and charm. I had interviewed many important people throughout my career, but I was rarely as intimidated as I felt sitting next to Miss Sarah Chandler.

As she talked, I couldn't help but notice her perfect white teeth because her smile was absolutely captivating. She was so knowledgeable and proud to share with me everything that she knew about the Billy Graham crusades. Talking about the massive crusades was definitely her specialty. She had traveled all over the world organizing the crusades and their enormous events.

I grinned because she talked with her hands as she spoke. She had long elegant fingers and beautiful soft hands. She was so poised, calm and full of grace that she kind of scared me. I had never met anyone like her before.

She did not wear a wedding ring so I assumed she too was single. I surprised myself when I ask her if she wanted to continue our interview while we grabbed something for dinner. She smiled her gracious smile and said, "Let me get my jacket first."

Sarah and I walked to a well-known hamburger restaurant three blocks away from the crusade. It was called the Burger House and they specialized in hamburgers, homemade fries and cherry cokes.

I got out my pen and notebook and before the food even arrived, I started writing down everything as fast as I could about Billy Graham. I learned that Billy Graham was born on November 7, 1918 in Charlotte, North Carolina. He had been raised on the family's dairy farm and he was the oldest of four children. His parents were strict Calvinists, but at the age of sixteen he attended a revival meeting of the evangelist Mordecai Hamm. Although, Billy was a well-behaved young man he was truly convicted by the preaching about sin in his life during that revival.

While we ate, she told me, "After reverend Graham graduated from High School he enrolled in a conservative Christian School, called Bob

Jones College. He soon transferred to Florida Bible Institute and while he was there, he joined a Southern Baptist Conservative Church. He was ordained as a minister in 1939 and after graduating he enrolled at Wheaten College to finish his spiritual training."

Sarah continued, "One of the very first sermons that he ever did was at the Bostwick Baptist Church, in Putnam, Florida. It was Easter Sunday and he was only eighteen years old. There were about forty people there and at the end of his sermon he had an alter call, and it surprised him because eleven people came forward."

Sarah got a strange smile on her face before going on, "It was there at Wheaten College that he met Ruth McCue Bell his future wife. Ruth's parents were missionaries and she had been raised in China until she was seventeen. Ruth and Reverend Graham had five children; Franklin, Anne, Ned, Gigi, and Ruth."

I studied Sarah's face as she talked, she was so joyful and easy to listen to. She seemed to know everything there was to know about Billy Graham and she didn't even use notes, but she delighted in sharing his life story with me. Everything she said was so positive and inspiring.

She continued on, "Then he joined Youth for Christ where he spoke to returning servicemen and young people about God. In 1947 he became president of the Northwestern School in Minnesota. In 1949 a group called "Christ for a Greater Los Angeles" ask him to speak at an L.A. revival. The revival lasted for eight weeks, and that's when the news media helped him to become kind of a Christian superstar."

Sarah went on to tell me, "Much of Billy Graham's success was related to the cultural climate of post WWII America. He helped bind together a hurting nation through religion and revival. Reverend Graham stated that either communism must die or Christianity must die, because he said it's actually a battle between Christ and anti-Christ. With the advent of nuclear weapons people turned to spirituality for comfort. He made evangelism look more trusting, and the media helped take his message to the masses."

She paused and just looked at me before going on, "I'm sorry, am I talking too fast?"

I shook my head back and forth, I didn't realize that I had been studying her so closely as she talked. She must have thought I wasn't listening, but actually I was listening intently, because I thought she was amazing. She no longer had her glasses on, and I could see her beautiful dark eyes and thick black lashes, and her eyes actually sparkled as she talked. She had flawless pale skin and her entire face just glowed with expression at each word she spoke. She had my undivided attention, but I could barely hear her talking. Then I realized I was no longer taking notes; that is why she questioned me. I took a deep breath and said, "Oh, I'm sorry, what were you saying?"

She grinned a sheepish grin at me before going on, "I said, to maintain a professional maturity Graham and his colleagues developed the Billy Graham Evangelistic Association, (BGEA.) He broadcast sermons over the radio on a program called the Hour of Decision. They started out with 150 stations and ended up on 1,200 stations across America. Eventually, the show became a television show and it was on for three years. They started publishing records, tapes, films and several books. BGEA created *Christianity Today* in 1955 and then the *Decision* magazine. They were soon published in Spanish, French and German."

I was beginning to feel a little jealousy towards this flawless man that she spoke so highly about, and I finally replied, "The Reverend Billy Graham seems almost perfect. How does he see himself after becoming so famous?" I kind of chuckled, "Is he bossy or arrogant or is he ever hard to get along with?"

"Oh, heavens no," she quickly defended. She got a strange look on her face before going on, and she softly said, "No the person that you see in Billy Graham, is the true person that he is. He loves teaching to massive crowds, but he continually surrounds himself with strong, Godly people. That helps keep him focused. One of his rules is that he will never be alone with any of the ladies. It is strictly against his beliefs, and that rule is strongly enforced."

She kind of laughed, "To answer your first question, he recognizes his flaws and he often gets upset with himself when he says the wrong things on television, or in an interview. He knows that he is constantly being scrutinized, and that some people are just waiting for him to mess up. Billy Graham is just an ordinary person that God has chosen to be a vessel to bring people to the Lord."

She got closer and looked me directly in the eyes, "You know Daniel, he is the most virtuous person that I have ever known. He is a true man of integrity." She went on, "He sees every person the same, and he loves every person the same. Every nationality, and every man, woman and child. Billy Graham has been put on the Gallup list of most admired people more times than any other man or woman in history. He has met with almost every President of the United States beginning with Harry S. Truman.

She smiled and stated, "He always tells us that Jesus did not come to earth to teach. He came to earth to die on the cross for our sins, and Jesus died on the cross for the sins of every one of us. He always says that when we die, we have a divine appointment. I have traveled with the group for over three years and I have to tell you, I have never met anyone like the Reverend Billy Graham."

The restaurant was starting to get noisier, and so we had to sit closer together to be able to hear each other talk. As we sat only inches from each other, looking face to face I felt an intimacy with Sarah that I have never felt with anyone before. She intrigued me in every possible way; her faith, her attitude, her intelligence, her confidence, and her abundant joy. She had an inner beauty that I had never seen in any other person.

My head felt foggy and I had a hard time concentrating, but I didn't want our conversation to come to an end. I thoroughly enjoyed being with Sarah. I lightly shook my head and took a short breath trying to think of something else to say, then I quickly blurted out, "Now, are you from Texas?"

She smiled and confidently shook her head back and forth and answered, "No, I was actually born on an army base in Georgia. My dad was in the army and my family traveled all over the world, but my father retired two years ago and they now live in a little town called Mountain Home. That's where he was stationed last. It's out in the middle of the desert, so I'm not sure why they call it Mountain Home. Have you ever heard of it?"

I quickly jumped up and shouted, "Mountain Home, Idaho?"

She laughed out loud, "Yes, it's in Idaho. Have you been there?"

I instantly sat back down and told her, "I live in Boise, Idaho. Thirty-nine miles west of Mountain Home."

Sarah grabbed both of my hands in hers and giggled, "You have got to be kidding me. You live thirty-nine miles from my parents? How strange," she giggled again as she put her hand over her mouth and apologized, "Oh I'm so sorry, I didn't mean to be insulting, I just didn't know that anyone else really lived in Idaho." She shyly grinned and quickly changed the subject, "Hey, I'm going home to see my parents in a few weeks. Maybe you can come see me while I'm there."

I joyfully laughed out loud, "Yes, I can show you all around Boise and the surrounding area. I have lived in Idaho all of my life, and my parents still live in the same house that I was raised in. In fact, it was the same house that my dad was raised in."

I continued on, "Of course, I no longer live at home. I live out on the bench, in a big apartment house with four other guys. All five of us travel a lot with our jobs, so we rarely even see each other. It works out well for all of us.

In fact, one of the guys is getting married in a few weeks, and I plan to be the best man at his wedding." I thought for a second and told her, "Bill and I have been best friends since grade school."

Sarah got an odd look on her face and she got really serious, "I would love to have you show me around your home town. I was joking with you earlier; my mom and Dad really like living in Idaho. Because I have lived so many places in my lifetime, I have always envied people who are very stable, have roots, and have friends from their childhood. Daniel, I went to seventeen different schools as I was growing up. I have friends from all over the world, but no one that I am really close to."

She just sat and stared at me for several seconds. When she finally spoke again, she said, "My dad loves to fish and hunt and both of my parents enjoy camping in their travel trailer. My parents say that after moving around so many times they like the peacefulness of Idaho. They love the beautiful mountains and the clear rivers and streams. They also like to snow ski and Mountain Home is only about a hundred miles away from the popular Sun Valley ski resort.

Sarah closed her eyes for a moment before adding, "Actually, they would like me to move home with them for a while because they think I have been working too much. Over the past three years I been all over the world setting up the crusades so that everything will be ready when the rest of the team arrives. My schedule is very hectic and they know I cannot keep this pace up forever."

She looked directly into my eyes and sadly told me, "I get tired of never having a permanent place to go home to. Everyone else in the group has a house and family someplace. They go on tour with the crusade and then they take a break and rest at home for several weeks."

She glanced down towards the floor before stating, "When I go see my parents, I plan to stay with them for a while. It was a difficult decision for me, but I won't be going with the crusade when it heads overseas next month."

I felt a strange sense of delight to hear that she would be staying in Idaho for a few weeks. I barely knew this woman, but I smiled at her and shyly stated, "You know you are such an easy person to talk too. I do a lot of interviews, but I think this has been one the most uncomplicated interviews that I have ever done. You are so honest and knowledgeable about everything."

When Sarah looked at me again, I could see a strange sadness in her eyes, and for some reason, I felt such an immediate closeness with her. I could just sense the overwhelming loneliness that she felt, I automatically put my hands over her hands to comfort her. This had definitely been a day of many life changing moments for me.

I attended the crusade every night for the remaining six days. I got everything that I needed to do my article about the incredible Reverend Billy Graham.

I was amazed at the magnificent dynamics that went into the production of a Billy Graham Crusade. Hundreds of people worked together to keep the crusades flawless, and Billy Graham never hesitated to let everyone know how much he appreciated their hard work and dedication. Sarah was right, Billy Graham never wavered. He was the same Godly person night after night.

Sarah and I went everywhere together throughout the rest of the crusade. We laughed a lot, we prayed together, and we could talk about anything. Being together seemed so natural, and I knew that I never wanted be alone again. By the end of the crusade my entire outlook on life had been redirected. From that time on serving God would be my top priority, and of course taking care of my beloved Sarah would be my second.

The Lord had not only sent me to Dallas to do a write up on The Reverend Billy Graham. He sent me there to restore my belief in Him and to meet my beautiful soulmate. Five months after we met, Sarah Joy Chandler became my bride. We were married at the Central Christian Church in downtown Boise. It was the same church that I had gone to for kindergarten and had been baptized in.

Sarah never went back with the Billy Graham Crusade group, but she often traveled with me before our four children were born. For the first time in her life she had a permanent home, real neighbors, loving church friends and she could be the room mother for each of our children. Sarah loved Boise, Idaho. Her new hometown was everything that she had ever dreamed it would be.

Seven

Ribbon Cutting Ceremony For the Twin Towers in New York

The World Trade center was originally planned to be constructed on the east side of Lower Manhattan. After months of changes, and debating it was finally built at the site of Radio Row in Lower West Side Manhattan, New York City.

Austin J. Tobin had a 30-year career as the executive Director of the Port Authority. He was the overseer of the original planning and development of the World Trade Center.

The concept of establishing a world trade center was partly inspired by the Rockefeller Center which had been developed in 1936. The 1939 New York World's Fair included an exhibit called the World Trade Center that was dedicated to the concept of "World peace through trade."

While searching for an architect to create this huge project the name Minoru Yamasaki came up. When Yamasaki received the offer to build the massive structure, he thought that it was a typo because the highest building he had ever constructed was the Michigan Consolidated Gas Company. It was only 30 stories high.

Minoru Yamasaki was a Detroit-based second-generation Japanese-American. He was known as a modernist mid-century architect. In the past, Yamasaki had used many Islamic forms in his buildings such as the Federal Science Pavilion at the Seattle World's Fair, and the Eastern Airlines terminal at Logan airport.

Yamasaki worked with structural engineers to come up with the revolutionary design: of two hollow tubes supported by closely spaced steel lattice.

One of the problems they encountered with constructing such a huge building was the limited space for elevators. They eventually decided on sky lobbies which are floors where people can switch from a large capacity express elevator to the 44th and 78th floors of each tower.

The sky lobby system in the Twin Towers created three separate connected elevator systems which would serve different segments of the building depending on which floor was chosen. It saved up to 70% of the space used for a traditional shaft. The large area that was saved was used as office space. The fastest elevators ran up to 1,700 feet per minute. When the towers were completed it would have 97 passenger elevators capable of carrying loads up to 10,000 pounds.

In May 1968 Lawrence Wien one of the owners of the Empire State Building ran an ad in the New York Times predicting that a commercial air liner was likely to fly into the towers during heavy fog. So, the towers had to be designed to be safe in case of such a collision. They tried to design the building against an impact of a fully, loaded 707 passenger jet, the largest plane that flew at that time.

The developers tried to prepare for an accidental air plane crashing into the building. After numerous arguments and many heated discussions, they estimated that the building could withstand the impact of a jet that would be traveling up to 600 mph. They tried to anticipate every problem that might occur with such tall buildings. (A terrorist attack was never mentioned.)

Minoru Yamasaki drew up the specific ideas for the twin towers and construction on the North Tower began in August 1968 and the South Tower in 1969. The Port Authority was not subject to local regulations and building codes for the city of New York, but the structural engineers ended up following draft versions of the1968 building code. It became the tallest building in the world, but within a year the Sears Tower in Chicago was finished and it was taller.

Europe imported pointed arches from Islam during the middle ages, and so non-Muslims have come to think of their innovations as the Gothic period.

Yamasaki had built the World Trade Center as a monument of Western Capitalism in the raiment of Islamic spirituality. Such mixing of the sacred and the profane is old hat to us. The Cass Gilbert Classic Woolworth Building, is dubbed the Cathedral to Commerce, and is decked in extravagant Gothic regalia.

The twin towers were swathed in a massive shimmering skin. Here Yamasaki was following the Islamic tradition of wrapping a powerful geometric form in a dense filigree. As in the inlaid marble pattern work of the Taj Mahal or the ornate carvings of the courtyard and domes of Alhambra. The shimmering filigree is the mark of the Holy. According to Oleg Grabar, the great American scholar of Islamic art and architecture the dense filigree alludes to a higher spiritual reality of Islam, and the shimmering quality of Islamic patterning relates to the veil that wraps the Kaaba at Mecca. Yamasaki courtyard mimicked Mecca's Assemblage of the holy sites.

The ground where the towers were to be constructed was largely landfill. The engineers would have to dig down 70 feet to reach bedrock as dirt and rock were removed. Concrete was poured with steel tips in a cage about two blocks wide and four blocks long. The cement cage was used to seal the basement and to keep the water from the Hudson Bay out from the foundation

To build the steel frames of the building they brought in Australian made 'Kangaroo cranes.' In all the towers were assembled from 200,000 pounds of steel. More than 10,000 workers were employed each day in building the World Trade Center.

It was an impressive melding of modern technology and traditional Islamic form. At the base of the towers Yamasaki used implied pointed arches. Derived from the characteristically pointed arches of Islam.

Yamasaki designed the world trade center plaza "a mecca;" to be a great relief from the narrow streets and sidewalks of the regular surrounding Wall Street area. He replicated the plan of Mecca's courtyard by creating a vast delineated square isolated from the city's bustle low column structures and capped by two perfectly square towers.

Around this same time period Yamasaki accepted three choice projects in Saudi Arabia; The Saudi Arabian Monetary Agency head office, The Eastern Province International Airport, and the King Fahd Royal Reception Pavilion. In all three projects he continued his exploration in melding traditional Islamic form with modern materials, methods and functions. The Saudis admired Yamasaki's designs so much that they put a picture of it on one of their bank notes.

When the Twin Towers were completed the World Trade Center was a large complex of seven buildings in Lower Manhattan, featuring the landmark Twin Towers. At the time of their completion, the original One World Trade Center was 1,368 feet tall and the Two World Trade Center was 1, 362 feet with a cost of $400 million dollars (equal to $2.27 billion today.) The first tenants moved into the North Tower in December 1970 and the South Tower in January 1972.

The iconic Twin Towers were a triumph of human imagination and will. When the project was completed the towers stood at 110 stories tall and could accommodate 50,000 workers and 200,000 visitors daily in its 10 million square foot of space. It was a symbol of New York City and Americas steadfast devotion to progress and the future.

My wife Sarah and I had only been married for a little over a year when I was asked to do a story about the ribbon cutting ceremony for the completion of the Twin Towers construction. The publisher requested a lot of pictures for this project so I took my photographer with us for some great magazine photos.

Within a few days the three of us had packed our bags, and we flew the 2,472 miles all the way across the United States to Lower West Side Manhattan.

We arrived in New York on April 2, 1973, two days before the dedication was to take place. The ribbon cutting ceremony was to be held on April 4, so we wanted to get there a little early and experience the excitement of the city before the day of the celebration.

The first thing that we noticed as our plane arrived in New York was the imposing new Twin Towers standing proudly amongst the exquisite New York skyline. Our photographer snapped several pictures from the plane as we flew past the beautiful new construction on our way to the airport to land. The impressive Twin Towers just seemed to glisten as the bright morning sunshine bounced off its shimmering outer coating.

Sarah and I had both seen New York before, but this time it was different, we were here for a triumphant occasion. We were here to do an article celebrating the completion of the Twin Towers.

On the day of the celebration the atmosphere was rather confusing to us. There was a lot of controversy about the new buildings. Apparently, many of the people of New York did not approve of the Twin Towers and the massive amounts of money that had been wasted on its construction.

Many were disillusioned because so many old buildings had been eliminated along Radio Row for the construction of the towers.

We read several disturbing articles in the local newspapers criticizing the celebration of the towers. When the time of the ribbon cutting ceremony finally occurred it had been raining constantly for several hours, and that alone would encourage many people to stay away.

We soon discovered that the President of the United States was no longer expected to come to do ribbon cutting ceremonies no matter how grand the ceremony would be. So, President Richard Nixon sent a statesman to be there in his place, but he too did not show up. The ceremony speech was delivered instead by the Port Authority Chairman.

To me the celebration that we witnessed was probably the most humbling and awe-inspiring in my career. Even with the controversy over the construction of the towers this was truly one of the most extraordinary dedications that I have ever witnessed.

When the Port Authority chairman told of the significance of the two towers the audience stood silently, in the pouring rain and strained to listen. The speaker stated that the Twin Towers were a magnificent symbol of the Nation's economic strength as well as the economic strength of the entire world.

The three of us, that had come all the way from Idaho, were truly honored to be there and witness this historical dedication in person. It was a day that none of us would ever forget.

Even with all of the mixed emotions throughout the city, I don't think I had ever been prouder of America than I was on that momentous day.

***

The finished construction of the World Trade Center was not completed until 1987, but six years after its completion on February 26, 1993, a bomb was detonated below the North Tower trying to bring down both towers. It was soon discovered that the World Trade Center was the target of a terrorist attack.

On Friday February 26, 1993, Ramzi, Yousef and some Jordanian friends drove a yellow Ryder van into Lower Manhattan and pulled into the public parking garage beneath the World Trade Center around noon. They parked on the underground B-2 level to explode their bomb.

The bomb was detonated with 1,336 pounds urea nitrate hydrogen gas. The enhanced device was intended to blow up the North Tower making it crash into the South Tower bringing down both towers and killing thousands. But the bomb was not powerful enough to destroy the towers as intended. Although it failed to destroy both towers the bomb killed six people and injured approximately a thousand others.

It wouldn't be until 1994 that the four men would be convicted on charges of conspiracy, explosive destruction of property, and the interstate transportation of explosives. By November 1997 two more would be convicted, and those two men, Ramzi and Yousef were found to be the masterminds behind the bombings.

Eight

Changes

In the mid-seventies advertising began to change. Intense pressures challenged the advertising business. Businesses were threatened by growing government regulations, but the government was forced to get involved to control all of the misleading tactics in American advertising. The public was beginning to get suspicious and disenchanted with every kind of advertising practice. Even though, the agencies were making continual efforts to increase diversity among advertising.

They often stretched the truth to sell their products. Advertising was getting so competitive that the companies were making accolades about their product that were out and out lies. Their product couldn't possibly do everything that they claimed it could do, but they tried everything to stay ahead of their competitors. When the advertisers discovered they could not say enough convincing remarks about their own products to keep them ahead of their competition, they tried stating bad, insulting remarks about their opposition. They would radically put down their adversary with extreme derogatory remarks. Some commercials were almost considered slanderous. With television, magazines, billboards and the computer industry there was daily changes in competition.

The practice of comparative advertising flourished. For example, many soft drink companies came up with catchy slogans to try to influence people to purchase their product over another soft drink product. Industry code review boards and federal government officials began to monitor the practices carefully. Often banning exaggerated or untrue claims or disparaging comments. The understanding and use of competition increased, revolutionizing countless facets of advertising.

Many company mergers occurred. In fact, by the end of the 1970's so many advertising companies had merged that there were no longer any major independent U.S. advertising agencies on the west coast.

U.S. advertising agencies began looking overseas for new markets and growth, and advertising unquestionably started to reform. Some agencies began getting criticized for using subliminal "sexual embedding."

Journalism professor Wilson Bryon Key accused Madison Avenue of placing "sex" somewhere in ads for potential companies or on magazine covers. Even on ads promoting things like Ritz crackers.

People became growingly suspicious and skeptical of advertising. In a 1976 Gallop Poll Americans were asked to rate honesty and ethical standards of those engaged in eleven fields of work. They found that the advertising executive rated the worst. He was the least to be trusted or believed.

Because of the severity of distrust of advertising, the FTC and National Advertising Review Board began holding ads to higher unprecedented standards of accuracy, honesty and disclosure, and advertising then started to change. The public had been misinformed so many times that there was little faith in advertising. People began questioning every advertisement that they saw or heard.

The film industry too was drastically changing. It was getting so corrupt and immoral that it was forced to take on a whole new rating system. For the first time in America's history the movie industry had to display what age group the movie being shown would be appropriate for.

The new movies had so much violence, graphic sex, bad language, and pornography that the theatre had to display its degree of obscenity. The ratings were G for general audience, PG for parental guidance, R and X for the worst. It was like our entire world had gone wild with absolutely no boundaries. Things were changing so rapidly there was no slowing it down.

The music industry was also radically changing. Music has always been a huge part of the American way of life, but the newer song lyrics seemed to be getting less and less restrictive. Throughout our history the language in songs had been monitored, censored and challenged, until now. By the end of the eighties and early nineties song writers began pushing everything to the limit until every offensive word or obscene gesture became accepted into the music arena.

The young people of this new generation were being exposed to language and insinuations that the earlier generations would have never repeated in public. The words that were once found offensive, were now being shouted and sung from center stage through the microphones and sound systems at every concert.

The majority of the young people in America were beginning to live two lives. They could be one person when they were home with their family, but their world was often in turmoil and uncertainty when they were around friends their own age. Their new generation had been exposed to heavy drugs, unrestricted sexual behavior, drinking, and shocking language like no other generation before. The innocence once reserved for the young, was gradually slipping away.

I was becoming somewhat overwhelmed with all of the widespread changes taking place. As a journalist and father, I began taking a more serious look at each article that I published. I double-checked for truth, honestly and credibility in every editorial that I wrote, because I couldn't believe some of the things that I had been witnessing.

I was amazed at how impetuously people were accepting the immoral changes of the world. In my interviews people would tell me such disturbing confessions, that I often felt I just couldn't listen anymore. I realized that the integrity of many successful business men, in every industry was being held hostage by their greed of money and success.

People whom I had known for years and I have always admired for their strong ethics and truthfulness were now becoming corrupt and disgraceful and sometimes even ending up in prison.

Their business practices had changed dramatically throughout the years, and they would do anything to stay ahead of their competitors, and keep their high-paying jobs. They were used to living at certain standards, and they were terrified of losing their big houses, private schools, and their private memberships at the best clubs.

The competition was so great, and the older executives that had arrived at the top of the success ladder were threatened by all of the new, young brilliant executives coming up ready to take their place. They felt forced to cut corners and purchase cheaper materials just to survive.

***

I was asked to write an article about the HIV virus in America. Hundreds of people were dying every day, and there was a big controversy as to when the virus had first come to United States and how it got here. Too many innocent people were being infected, and there had been little information given to the public about why it had become such a pandemic, and people were confused.

I was contacted because the doctors and science researchers felt that it was time to bring some of the data and information that they had collected out in the open, so that society could become more knowledgeable. A lot of false information had been given out and people were terrified of what they had heard. Hours of research had been devoted to the HIV and Aids project and it was time for people to know the truth about what the researchers had found.

For this project I would need to travel to Duke University Hospital in Durham, N.C. There I would be doing research at the Duke University Health System Clinical Laboratories. It is the best college of American Pathologist accredited. It has the state-of-the-art multidisciplinary Lab. In North Carolina, I would be able to interview doctors and the pathologists who had been working directly with the HIV research program.

I knew that I would be away from home for a few days, but the doctors working on this project felt the information was critical. It was time for the truth to come out. I was hesitant to do this study because this project was very serious, and it was something I knew nothing about.

My wife Sarah and I tried not to judge the way other people lived their lives. As long as their lifestyle did not affect us, we paid little attention to how they lived theirs.

We have always been very active in our church, and in all of our children's school activities, and raising our family has extensively been the main focus of our life.

I was personally chosen for this project, but because of my growing family I have recently become very selective of what I write about. Yet, at the same time, I found the HIV project kind of thought-provoking because it was just one more element that was drastically transforming this new world that I had been raising my family in.

The HIV virus has affected thousands of households in the United States alone, so perhaps, I should become more knowledgeable about its origin. This was a very important assignment, and they had chosen me because of my ethics and integrity, and no matter what I discovered they knew that I would only write the truth.

After arriving in North Carolina, I first interviewed several doctors and then I was sent to the Duke Clinical Laboratories to follow up on the documentation. The documents that I read stated that hunters in Africa first came in contact with HIV through infected chimpanzees. Somehow the blood of the infected chimps transferred into the cuts or wounds of the hunters. As early as the 1920's HIV had been labeled a global pandemic. I found that countless investigations showed that something was mysteriously killing gay men. Most of the studies tied the HIV virus back to their lifestyle.

By the late seventies it was discovered that many cases had been transferred through human blood transfusions, and by infected needles shared by drug users. The AIDS virus was now also affecting many heterosexual men and women, as well as children.

HIV had actually been spreading to a large number of people for several years, even before AIDS was ever identified. The discoveries that I found unanimously conferred that the virus came from the Caribbean to New York in the 1970's.

The LGBT had gained recognition back in the 1950's when the Mattachine Society was formed. It was formed by a man by the name of Harry Hay a prominent gay-rights activists, communists, labor advocate, and Native American civil rights campaigner.

In my research, I also discovered that in the year 1978 a small group called Gay Pride marched in San Francisco as well as Los Angeles. By the next year, in 1979 about 75,000 people participated in the National march for lesbian and gay rights in Washington D.C.

By 1984 fourteen private bath houses and private sex clubs in San Francisco that catered to homosexuals were closed. They were closed due to the high-risk of spreading AIDS.

In October of 1985 the actor Rock Hudson died of AIDS. He was the first high-profile fatality. He left $250,000 to set up the American Foundation for AIDS research. By the year 1989 there was an estimated 400,000 cases of AIDS worldwide.

The AIDS epidemic brought years of suffering for those effected and their families. It also ushered in a revolution in attitudes that has allowed us to talk about sexuality more frankly than we ever did before.

Those discussions soon led to gay rights, white rights, black rights, women's rights, green rights, and of course children's rights. This would eventually open the door to sexual orientation, gender identity, bisexuals, transgenders and gay marriage.

Around this same time in the nation's history our American way of life was drastically changed when the Supreme court ruled 7 to 2 to give women the right to end the life of their unborn babies by abortion. Often times the men were left completely out of the decision choices once abortion became legal. Legalizing abortion was a very difficult ruling for many Americans.

In this research article I also discovered that all of these radical changes had taken a drastic toll on the families of America. The divorce rate had skyrocketed, leaving broken homes and confused children in its wake. As a result, many men and women stopped getting married at all, because they feared divorce.

Even the popular sitcoms that were on television at that time were aimed at young single people living a carefree one-night-stand consenting relationship. Well-liked comedy shows like Seinfeld and Friends gave the new generation their approval that sleeping together on the first date was normal and sometimes even expected.

Young couples soon discovered it was much more convenient if they just lived together and raised their children. The mother wanted to keep the child, but neither her or the boyfriend wanted to make any permanent commitment. As a single mother, the woman could receive lower housing cost, subsidized day care, free insurance for her family, and food stamps, all at the government's expense.

It became very common for single moms and dads to have two or three children and never get married. The system worked out well for everybody. People would live together for six or seven years, the children would have the father's last name, the mother and father both lived in the same house together, and raised the children, and the government was there to help with expenses. After a few years if the parents parted ways there were no legal fees to pay. Both parties just walked away; no ties.

Apparently, it had become so accepted to just live together, that statistics show that 1 in 4 couples between the ages 18 to 34 began buying a house together without ever being married. They both sign for the property because they usually need both incomes to qualify for the loan, and because this has become so normal, a Cohabitation Agreement was developed to protect both buyers.

All of these lifestyle changes were rapidly transforming the America that I knew and loved. But as I was looking through the research documents for all of my clarifications, I came across an even more disturbing newspaper headline editorial. It was a recent scandalous report pertaining to the current President of the United States.

The office of the President of the United States of America was dishonored and in total disgrace when President Bill Clinton was caught having a sexual affair inside the oval office with a young twenty-two-year-old White House intern.

The intern, Monica Lewinsky was born in San Francisco to a well-to-do family and was raised in the Los Angeles area. The article stated that the President and Miss Lewinsky first got together that November when many of the White House staffers were furloughed during a federal government shutdown. Lewinsky was allowed to keep working because she was not on the payroll. During that time, she met the President and that is when they started their first sexual encounter.

The President and Miss Lewinsky continued with their affair for months and they met in the oval office regularly. They showed total disrespect to the office of the President of the United States or to the American people that he served.

The affair was finally exposed when Miss Lewinsky confessed her involvement to a coworker, Linda Tripp. Tripp then privately taped some of the conversations that she had with Miss Lewinsky. Soon Lewinsky's continual visits drew suspicion from people in the administration, and their private phone calls were secretly recorded.

The affair with Miss Lewinsky went public, and at first the President denied ever being with Monica Lewinsky, but he later admitted to the affair after evidence proved him guilty. The house of representatives impeached the President for perjury, and obstruction of justice.

It was then discovered that another young female government employee, Paula Jones had filed charges a few years earlier against President Bill Clinton, when he was still the governor of Arkansas.

The mainstream media picked up on the stories and a shocking scandal occurred. President Clinton went on national television and apologized for his behavior. Then he just went on to finish his second term in the white house. Astonishingly, when he left the White House, he left with strong public opinion approval ratings, despite all of the scandals.

It is not my position to be judgmental of any person's lifestyle or beliefs, but after researching this insightful information I could no longer ignore the problems that were taking place in my country. I knew that with all of the changes around me, eventually every one of us would be affected.

The information that I found for these articles reminded me of a statement I recently read that was written by an unknown author. It said "We are now living in a generation where the sin that once snuck secretly down the back alley, now struts proudly down the main street."

Nine

September 11, 2001

On September 11, 2001 the comfortable America that we know and love was instantly turned into a vulnerable combat zone. The Islamic extremist terrorist group al-Qaeda ruthlessly killed thousands of people when they flew two planes into the Twin Towers in New York City. It was the worst terrorist attack ever achieved on American soil. al-Qaeda was a recognized international terrorist network that was funded by Osama Bin Laden.

In the late 1980's, al-Qaeda had targeted both civilians and soldiers in other serious attacks around the world. At that time, it was reported that al-Qaeda wanted to get rid of all Western American influence in Muslim countries and set up an extreme form of Islamic rule across the world.

In 1998 Osama Bin Laden issued a fatwa entitled "Declaration of War Against the Americans occupying the Land of two Holy Places." The document was signed by Osama Bin Laden and several others calling for the killing of Americans. It was a long document, and it states disapproval of American activities in numerous countries. It was faxed to supporters across the world. It called for American troops to leave Saudi Arabia, and Osama Bin Laden declared a holy war against the United States.

Many Islamic scholars stated that Bin Laden was angry because he thought the Islamic world had fallen behind the Western world. When the Twin Towers were completed in New York City in 1973 America stated that it was a magnificent symbol of America's economic strength and the economic strength of the rest of the world.

Al-Qaeda complained that for over several years the United States has been occupying the lands of Islam in the holiest of places. Bin Laden was upset because the United States gave support to Israel. Through the al-Qaeda terrorist network Bin Laden could provide both leadership and financial support for any planned terrorist attack. He was the one who selected both of the experienced jihadists that were sent to America for the Twin Towers attack.

In mid-January 2000, two men arrived in the United States. In the Spring of 2000, they both took flying lessons in San Diego, California. They both spoke English, but they performed poorly with their flying lessons and eventually they served as secondary leaders and others were chosen.

Finally, Bin Laden chose two different men because they could speak good English and they already had their commercial pilot license. The first one that he chose bragged that he could help the other hijackers blend in by teaching them how to order food, and dress like westerners.

Some of the hijackers received passports from corrupt Saudi officials who knew family members that lived in America. Others just used fraudulent passports to gain entry. Most of the terrorists had only been to the United States on this one occasion, and by the time the attack took place, they had been here approximately 3 to 4 months.

NASA intercepted a telephone conversation a short time before the attack, so they knew that something 'big' was going down. They alerted the CIA, but they did not alert the FBI.

By January the senior council terrorist official Richard Clarke and the CIA director George Tenet had been alerted that a major attack was about to come about, but they thought that the attack would be in Saudi Arabia or Israel.

In early July, Clarke put out the "domestic agency on full alert signal" telling them that something big was about to happen soon. He then asked the FBI and State Department to alert the ambassadors and all police departments to go to "Threat Delta." Clarke later wrote that somewhere in the CIA reports there was information that two known al-Qaeda terrorist had come into the U.S.

The FBI then got information that strange things had been going on at several of the flight schools in the U.S., but none of that information ever got to the white house.

On July 13, 2001, a CIA agent wrote a memo requesting permission to inform the FBI, but they never responded.

On August 6, 2001, at the CIA's Presidential Daily Briefing a private memo designated "For the President's eyes only" stated Osama Bin Laden is determined to strike the U.S.

Early on the morning of September 11, 2001 nineteen hijackers took control of four commercial airliners. The Boeing 757 and the Boeing 767 in route to California, took off from Logan International Airport in Boston, Massachusetts. They chose large planes with long flight patterns because they would be full of people and fuel for a long trip.

Osama Bin Laden chose to attack the World Trade Center, out of all of the buildings in New York because the towers were the tallest in the city. Also, because the buildings were filled with hundreds of people and it was designed to be a center of American and global commerce. The World Trade Center was not just a tall building it was proof that New York believed in itself at a time when New York's future seemed uncertain.

It was later discovered that Osama Bin Laden may have had a more personal motivation for destroying the Twin Towers. The World Trade Center's architect Minoru Yamasaki was a favorite designer of the Bin Laden family. It is well-known that the Bin Laden's were involved with almost all royal construction in Saudi Arabia, and Yamasaki had designed most of the large structures there. Minoru Yamasaki was an architect who merged modernism with Islamic influences.

Bin Laden could see how Yamasaki had clothed the World Trade Center, a monument of Western Capitalism on the remnant of Islamic Spirituality. It was said that to Bin Laden the World Trade Center was not only an International landmark, but also a fake idol.

There were several photographers taking pictures in the New York area at the exact time that the first plane hit the towers. One of those photographers was David Monderer. Mr. Monderer had been waiting each day for the perfect sunlight so that he could get a flawless photograph of the New York skyline. At 8:30 a.m. on September 11, 2001 he got that perfect picture. As he snapped one photograph after another, American Airlines Flight 11 flew directly into the North Tower of The World Trade Center, and he caught all of the horror and destruction on film precisely as it happened.

Earlier that morning at 7:59 a.m., American Airlines flight 11, a Boeing 767 with 92 people aboard took off from Boston's Logan International airport on route to Los Angles.

At 8:14 a.m., United Airlines Flight 175, a Boeing 767 with 65 people on board took off from Boston also headed for Los Angeles.

At 8:19 a.m., flight attendants on board Flight 11 alerted ground personnel that the plane had been hijacked.

At 8:20 a.m., American Airlines Flight 77 takes off from Dulles International Airport outside of Washington, D.C. The Boeing 757 is headed to Los Angeles with 64 people on board.

At 8:24 a.m., the hijacker Mohammed Atta makes the first of two accidental transmissions from Flight 11 to ground control. Apparently, he was trying to communicate with the plane's cabin.

By 8:40 a.m., The Federal Aviation Administration (FAA) alerts North American Aerospace Defense Command (NORAD)'s North east Air Defense Sector (NEADS) about the suspected hijacking of Flight 11. In response, NEADS scrambles two fighter planes that are located at Cape Cod's Otis Air National Guard Base to locate and tail Flight 11. They were not even in the air yet when Flight 11 crashed into the North Tower.

At 8:41 a.m., United Airlines Flight 93, a Boeing 757 with 44 people aboard takes off from Newark International Airport on route to San Francisco, California. It had been scheduled to depart at 8:00 a.m., around the time of the other hijacked flights.

By 8:46 a.m., Mohammed Atta and the other hijackers aboard American Airlines Flight 11 crash the plane between floors 93 and 99 of the North Tower of the World Trade Center killing everyone on board the plane and hundreds of people inside of the building.

At 8:47 a.m., within seconds, NYPD and FDNY forces dispatch units to the World Trade Center while the Port Authority Police Department officers on site began immediate evacuation of the North Tower.

By 8:50 a.m., the White House Chief of Staff, Andrew Card alerts President George W. Bush that a plane has hit the World Trade Center. The President was visiting an elementary school in Sarasota, Florida at the time.

At 9:02 a.m., after initially instructing tenants of the World Trade Center South Tower to remain in the building, Port Authority Officials broadcasts orders to evacuate both towers via the public address system. An estimated 10,000 to 14,000 people were already in the process of evacuating.

By 9:03 a.m., hijackers crash United Airlines Flight 175 into floors 75 through 85 of the World Trade Center's South Tower. Killing everyone on board and hundreds inside the building.

By 9:08 a.m. the FAA bans all take off flights going to New York City or through the airspace around the city.

By 9:21 a.m., the Port Authority closes all bridges and tunnels in the New York City area.

At 9:24 a.m., the FAA notifies NEADS of the suspected hijacking of Flight 77 after some passengers and crew aboard are able to alert family members on the ground.

At 9:31 a.m., one hour and thirty minutes after the first plane took off from Boston's International Airport, President George W. Bush spoke from Florida. He then calls the event in New York City an "apparent terrorist attack on our country."

At 9:37 a.m., the hijackers aboard Flight 77 crash the plane into the Western facade of the Pentagon in Washington, D.C. killing 59 people aboard the plane and 125 military and civilians inside the building.

At 9:42 a.m., for the first time in history the FAA grounds all flights over or bound for the Continental United States. Over the next two and a half hours, some 3,300 commercial flights and 1,200 private planes are guided to land at airports in Canada and the United States.

By 9:45a.m., there are rumors escalating of other attacks around the nation so the White House and U.S. Capitol building are evacuated along with many other high-profile buildings, landmarks and public spaces.

By 9:59 a.m., only 56 minutes after being hit, the North Tower of the World Trade Center collapses.

At 10:07 a.m., after passengers and crew members aboard the hijacked Flight 93 contacted friends on the ground, and learn about the attacks in New York and Washington, they mount an attempt to retake the plane. In response the hijackers deliberately crash the plane into a field in Somerset County, Pennsylvania. Killing all 40 passengers and crew aboard.

By 10:20 a.m., because of the slow and confused communication from the FAA officials, only Flight 11 had been warned about being hijacked. At 10:20 a.m., Vice President Dick Cheney issued orders to shoot down any commercial aircraft that could not be identified. The instructions were not relayed in time for the fighter pilots to take action. Some fighters took to the air without live ammunition, knowing that to prevent the hijackers from striking their intended targets they would be forced to ram their fighter jets into the side of the commercial aircraft, immediately after ejecting from their planes.

For the first time in U.S. history SCATANA was evoked stranding thousands of passengers across the world. The United States airspace was closed to international flights, and it caused hundreds of people to be turned back or to be redirected. Canada received 226 of the diverted flights.

Many businesses across the United States immediately closed after the attack. They were waiting to find the intentional nature of the events to become clear before reopening for business. It was safer to close down all monuments and skyscrapers than to take a chance on further strikes.

Operation Yellow Ribbon was enforced to deal with the large number of grounded planes and stranded passengers.

At 10:28 a.m., The World Trade Center South Tower collapses. Just 102 minutes after being struck by Flight 11.

By 11:00 a.m., Mayor Rudy Giuliani calls for the evacuation of Lower Manhattan south of Canal Street, including more than 1 million residents, workers and tourists. Efforts continued throughout the afternoon to search for survivors at the World Trade Center site.

At 1:00 p.m., from a U.S. military base in Louisiana, President Bush announces that the U. S. military forces are on high alert worldwide.

At 2:51 p.m., the U.S. navy dispatches missile destroyers to New York and Washington, D.C.

Buildings 4, 5, 6 and 7 had been burning since the attack and at 5:20 p.m., the 47 story Seven World Trade Center collapses after burning for several hours. The building had been evacuated in the morning and there were no casualties, though the collapse forced rescuers to flee for their lives.

By midday, the U. S. had intercepted multiple communications pointing to Osama bin Laden.

By 6:58 p.m., President Bush returned to the White House after he first stops at military bases in Louisiana and in Nebraska.

At 8:30 p.m., President George W. Bush addresses the nation, calling the attacks "evil, despicable acts of terror" and declaring that America and its friends and allies would "stand together to win the war against terrorism."

A good portion of the power went out in the Manhattan area at the time of the attack and many subways and tunnels had been stopped and had to be evacuated. All of the phone lines were jammed and no calls could get through. September 11, 2001, was definitely a day of tremendous grief and confusion.

After the attack, New York City looked like a war zone, all of the events had transpired so quickly that people were scrambling for their lives. Most people could not even comprehend what had happened. They were in shock and they were running in every direction, but they soon remembered they had nowhere to run, because Manhattan is an island with water on every side.

All transportation was shut down within one minute after the first plane hit. The entire town was in total lockdown, halting all buses, subways and commuter rails as well as roadways, bridges and tunnels. The authorities were trying to prevent any further attacks.

Many boats that were in the harbor at that time witnessed the billowing smoke and destruction taking place in Manhattan and they instantly headed to shore to help people get off of the island. Crews aboard ferries, fishing boats, and tour boats joined mariners of all kinds to launch an unplanned evacuation. There had never been an emergency plan ever created to evacuate Manhattan before that day, but within minutes every type of watercraft nosed their boats up to the sea wall and began the massive rescue to get the hordes of people out of Manhattan.

All of the escapees were covered in soot and ash from the burned, collapsed buildings. They looked like "gray ghosts" covered in powder plaster. It was total chaos, the boats picked up small children without their parents and several terrified animals. Some of the people impatiently waiting became completely overwhelmed with fear, and they began senselessly jumping into the water. The current swiftly began pulling them out toward the sea, but the smaller boats practiced their "Man Overboard" drills and rescued the swimmers from the water.

Soon boats and ferries of every size arrived and picked up people who had waited on the shore. Any type of water craft that was close by came to help get the people to safety.

Everyone was so desperate to get off of the island that they were stacked ten or more deep, smashed up against the railings along the water's edge. Throughout the day approximately 150 different vessels continued to cross the mile of the Hudson River dropping passengers off at ferry terminals in Weehawken, a triage center in Jersey City and slips in parks, marinas and yacht basins, as well as makeshift docking places all along the New Jersey waterfront. Within 9 hours the vessels had evacuated over 500,000 people from Manhattan. Many compared the 9/11 rescue to the May 1940 Dunkirk Mission in world War II.

There was madness on one side, and people trying to help other people on the other side. Within hours after the attack, police and rescue workers from around the country took leave from their jobs and traveled to New

York to help rescue bodies. Blood donations surged in the weeks after 9/11 following the attack.

After the attack, there was heightened security throughout the New York area. Wall Street was closed until the 17th of September. Bridges and tunnels were closed to non-emergency vehicles in all directions. Deliveries of food and perishables were canceled and left to rot, leading to a shortage in restaurants and grocery stores.

2,906 people were killed at the World Trade Center including 19 hijackers, and 6,000 people were injured. 265 people were killed in the four planes including the terrorists. 43 members of the city fire department and 71 law enforcement officers were lost in the World Trade Center, and 55 military and 125 civilian personnel were killed in the Pentagon. This was the deadliest terrorist attack in world history and the most devastating attack on the United States since the attack on Pearl Harbor on December 7, 1941.

Within days people streamed into New York from neighboring cities and states to try to help and restore sanity to the distraught area. Scenes of horror of rubble and bodies was contrasted with signs of hope and defiance as American flags were raised above the carnage.

People posted photos of missing friends and family members that had not been found. They placed the loved one's pictures on a wall for everyone to see. Hoping in desperation that their loved ones may show up alive. The city pulled together in a way that had never been seen before. People stood in lines on the sides of the streets and cheered the National Guard and rescue workers as they worked near what was now known as "Ground Zero."

All over America people flew flags out their car windows and in the bed of their trucks. You constantly saw flags in every yard and business. American's were more patriotic after the 9/11 attack than they had ever been before. Osama bin Laden tried to take down America, but instead

American united even stronger. The approval ratings of President George W. Bush soared to around 90%.

The United States enacted the Homeland Security Act of 2002 creating the Department of Homeland Security. The U.S. also passed the U.S.A. Patriot Act saying it would help detect terrorism and other crimes against the United States.

By 2002, the 9/11 Commission would be created to study the events leading up to September 11th and provide recommendations for emergency preparedness and response. Many observers criticized the Intelligence Community for numerous "intelligence failures" as one of the major reasons the attack was not prevented.

It was later discovered that the terrorists had used mace, tear gas and pepper spray to overcome the attendants, and some of the people on board had even been stabbed.

Mohammed Atta was identified as one of the hijackers when his luggage was left behind at Boston's Logan International Airport. The luggage failed to make it aboard American Airlines Flight 11. The papers inside the abandoned luggage contained all of the of the hijacker's names, and their detailed assignments and their al-Qaeda connections.

By September 27, 2000, they released photos and ID's of the nineteen hijackers. Fifteen were from Saudi Arabia, two were from United Arab Emirates, one was from Egypt and another man was from Lebanon. After the attack Bin Laden and his partner in crime, Ayman al-Zawahiri recorded videotapes and audio recordings, telling why they orchestrated the attack. Bin Laden discussed the organized attack and he spoke of being angry because of the U.S. support for Israel. Although, most of the writings that Bin Laden sent showed his disdain for President Bush, he also stated that he had hoped to destroy and bankrupt the entire United States during the Twin Towers attack.

Osama Bin Laden sent a letter stating that the idea of destroying the Twin Towers had first occurred to him when he witnessed Israel's bombardment of the high-rise apartment buildings during the 1982 Lebanon War many years earlier.

Bin Laden and Ayman al-Zawahiri soon released additional video tapes and audio recordings stating that Bin Laden interpreted Mohammed as wanting to ban the permanent presence of Infidels in America. Osama bin Laden wanted to totally get rid of all western American influence in America, and also in every Muslim country.

A massive search and rescue operation continued at the Twin Tower's location for several weeks, and the fires continued to burn in the debris of the destroyed buildings. Many citizens held the view that the assault on the Twin Towers "would change our world forever."

The Bush administration announced a War on Terrorism, with a goal of bringing Osama bin Laden and al-Qaeda to justice. They wanted to prevent the emergence of any other terrorist networks. There were economic and military sanctions placed against states perceived as harboring terrorists and increasing global surveillance and sharing intelligence.

Shortly, after September 11th U. S. officials speculated the possible involvement of Saddam Hussein. Although, unfounded, the association contributed to public support for the invasion of Iraq.

On October 7, 2001 the war, in Afghanistan began with the U.S. and British forces initiating aerial bombing campaigns in Afghanistan targeting the Taliban and al-Qaeda camps. Later, they invaded Afghanistan with ground troops of special forces. This was the second largest operation of the U.S. Global War on terrorism outside the U.S., and the largest directly connected to terrorism.

For a short time, the September 11th attack awakened the country to the fact that the weak immigration enforcement had presented a huge vulnerability that terrorist can exist within our nation undetected. But, immediately, after opening the hunt for Osama bin Laden President Bush visited the Islamic Center of Washington and asked the public to view Arabs and Muslims living in the U.S. as American patriots. The attack had made people very suspicious of all Arabs and Muslims, and the Muslims feared for their lives.

Because the President was so adamant about the American people not targeting the Muslims living in America, the pendulum began to swing completely the other way. Many American's embraced the Muslims and the Muslim beliefs, oftentimes ignoring our own nations principles so we didn't offend the rights of other religions. None of the American people wanted to be labeled a bigot or to appear prejudiced or offend anyone, so after 9/11 we began to break away from the Christian ideals that this nation was founded on.

A federal technical building and fire safety litigation of the collapsed Twin Towers was put together by the U. S. Department of Commerce and the National Institute of Standards and Technology. They were hired to investigate the building's construction and the materials used.

The reports concluded that the fireproofing on the Twin Towers steel infrastructure was blown off by the initial impact of the planes. If this had not occurred, the towers would likely have remained standing. The fire weakened the trusses supporting the floors making the floor sag. The sagging floors pulled on the exterior steel columns to the point where the exterior columns bowed inward. With the core columns damaged the building's buckling exterior columns could no longer support the buildings, causing them to collapse. Also, the tower's stairways were not adequately reinforced to provide an emergency escape for people above the impact zone.

The Inspector General of the CIA conducted an interview of the CIA's performance and harshly criticized the Senior CIA officials for not doing everything possible to confront terrorism including trying to stop the two main hijackers and for failing to share information with the FBI. "This is how the battles began," wrote the New York Times.

For several months after the attack, our nation rallied together. People were exceedingly patriotic. They powerfully united together to fight against the terrorist who had invaded our soil. As never before we were truly one nation under God. America's patriotism was stronger than I had ever witnessed in my lifetime.

Then slowly the unison started to fade, and people seemed to forget why they had united together in the first place. The car flags gradually disappeared and our world seemed to take a different turn. The American people once again began to voice their opinions, and they were distraught and frustrated. Within a few months the shock had worn off, and the shock was replaced with rage; rage towards authority, and towards the unknown.

The American people had always lived their lives the way they had chosen to live, and they were tired of feeling caged, and afraid. Americans loved to travel, they love to fly, eat in expensive restaurants, and go to the theatre, and for months after 9/11 this was all taken away. Their lives had been disrupted, and they were determined to take their freedom back.

The news media had reported about the mishandling of intelligence information before the 9/11 attack, and people became upset that our government had allowed this atrocity to ever happened to us in the first place.

Ten

Harold Frederick Shipman Doctor Death

Harold Frederick Shipman was born on the Bestwood Council Estate in Nottingham, England of the United Kingdom. He was the second of four children born to Harold Frederick Shipman, a lorry driver and Vera Brittan a homemaker and mother. His entire family were devout Methodists. When he was a young man, he was an accomplished rugby player in a youth league. He was also an excellent long-distance runner and he served as the vice-captain of the youth athlete's team.

Harold was the favorite child of his domineering mother. As he got older, he spent less time with young people his own age and more and more time with his mother.

They often went places alone. Even after his younger siblings came along, he was the child she always chose to take with her where ever she went. At an early age, she instilled in him a sense of superiority that tainted most of his later relationships, leaving him an adolescent with few friends.

One day tragedy struck the Shipman family when Harold's mother was diagnosed with terminal lung cancer. Harold idolized his mother, so when she needed someone to care for her, he willingly sat by her side.

When his mother started to decline, she was given morphine for the severe pain. Harold became fascinated by the positive effect that morphine had on his dying mother. During her last days he wouldn't leave her side; he was unfailingly attentive to her every need.

His mother died on June 21, 1963; Harold was barely seventeen years old. He was absolutely devastated by her death, for days after the funeral he sat in a dark corner moping, and he wouldn't leave the house. Within a few weeks after her death he decided that he wanted to go to medical school. He was admitted to Leeds University Medical School for training two years later. He failed his exams the first time, and he needed to pass them before he could begin his hospital internship. The second time he passed, and he was accepted to Leeds University.

He was still very much a loner, but he met his future wife on a double decker bus as he was riding back and forth to the University. He had only known his future wife for a short while, and when they got married, he was nineteen and his new bride was seventeen, and five months pregnant with their first child. He married his wife Primrose May Oxtoby on November 5, 1966, and he became a working physician in 1970.

By 1974 he was the father of two and had joined a medical practice in Todmorden, Yorkshire where he virtually thrived as a family practitioner before allegedly becoming addicted to the painkiller Pethidine. He forged prescriptions for large amounts of the drug and he was forced to leave his practice in 1975 when he was caught by his medical colleagues. At that time, he entered a drug rehab program, and received a small fine and a conviction of forgery.

A few years later Shipman was accepted onto the staff at Donnybrook Medical Center in Hyde, where he ingratiated himself as a hardworking doctor who enjoyed the trust of patients and colleagues alike. By then he had four children and appeared to have truly settled down.

Dr. Shipman had a reputation for arrogance amongst the junior staff, but his patients loved him, and he remained on staff there for the next two decades. His sometimes, snobbish behavior incurred only minor interest from the other health care professionals that he worked with. He was a popular doctor, and so no one on staff cared about his egotistical personality. They figured it was just who he was.

His practice was thriving, but one day the local undertaker noticed that Dr. Shipman's patients seemed to be dying at an unusually high rate. He also noticed that they all seemed to exhibit similar poses in death. Most of his dead patient were fully clothed, and sitting up or reclining on a settee.

The undertaker was concerned enough to approach Shipman about it directly. When the undertaker questioned the doctor about these strange coincidences, Shipman didn't seem the least bit concerned or offended. Dr. Shipman reassured the undertaker that there was nothing to worry about, and because of the doctor's nonchalant attitude, no one else was contacted about the situation at that time.

Later, another colleague, a doctor by the name of Dr. Susan Booth, also found the similarities disturbing, and she told the local coroner's office, who contacted the police.

A covert investigation followed, but Shipman was cleared as it appeared that his records were in order. The inquiry failed to contact the General Medical Council, or the Criminal Records department. Later, a more thorough investigation revealed that Shipman had been altering his medical records of his patients to corroborate their cause of death.

In March, Dr. Linda Reynolds of Donnybrook Surgery in Hyde, along with the people who worked at the funeral parlor expressed their concerns to the coroner about the high death rate among Shipman's patients. They were particularly concerned about the number of cremation forms for his elderly women patients that he had needed countersigned. The matter was brought to the attention of the police who were unable to find sufficient evidence to charge the doctor at that time.

It was later discovered that in April 1998 when the police had been forced to abandoned the evidence against Shipman, that he proceeded to kill three more people a short time after they had confronted him. By May it seemed that Shipman was no longer in touch with reality, because he continued to kill his patients even after he knew that the police were watching him.

His last victim was Kathleen Grundy who was found dead at her home on June 24, 1998. Kathleen Grundy was very prominent, and she had been the mayoress of Hyde. She was 81 years old, but she was very fit and healthy. On June 24, 1998 Dr. Shipman visited her at her cottage for what she thought was to be a routine blood test. Instead of drawing blood he gave her a lethal dose of morphine.

Her friends found her dead later that morning. She was fully dressed and sitting up on a sofa. It was soon discovered that Dr. Shipman was the last person to see her. He also signed her death certificate and recorded old age as her cause of death.

When the accusations against the popular doctor first came out, people were appalled. Most people saw him as a loving family man and a competent doctor. He was a very respected member of the community. They would never suspect that any criminal charges could ever be filed against him. In fact, in the beginning, his patients stood up for him and continually denied the horrifying rumors that were being told about him.

At the time the investigation began, Dr. Shipman's practice saw over 3,000 patients. Many of his patients had been seeing him for years, and they suspected nothing. Hiding behind his status as a caring family doctor, it was almost impossible to establish exactly why Shipman would be killing his patients, or even how many he had killed.

Dr. Harold Frederick Shipman often known as 'Fred" was a very typical looking man, not someone you would ever suspect to be a killer. He appeared honest, thoughtful and intelligent, and he was a very competent doctor. Harold was tall, muscular built and he dressed very stylish in his dark suit, his crisp shirt and tie and well-shined shoes. The doctor wore glasses and a full beard, and mustache, and he walked with an air of confidence. Most people would even consider him to be quite handsome, he certainly didn't look like your normal murder suspect.

From the very beginning he denied all of the charges, and did nothing to assists the authorities. Indeed, his killing spree was only brought-to-an-end thanks to the determination of Angela Woodruff, the daughter of Kathleen Grundy. She refused to accept the explanations given for her mother's death.

Her mother, Kathleen Grundy was an energetic, wealthy 81-year-old widow. She was found dead at her home on June 24, 1998 following an earlier visit by Dr. Shipman.

Angela Woodruff was advised by Shipman that an autopsy was not required and Kathleen Grundy was buried in accordance with her daughter's wishes. Angela was a lawyer and she had always handled her mother's affairs, so she was quite surprised when she discovered that another will had been written, leaving the bulk of her mother's estate to Dr. Harold Shipman. Woodruff was convinced that the documents were a forgery and that Shipman had murdered her mother, forging the will to benefit from her death.

Angela Woodruff alerted the local police where Detective Superintendent Bernard Postles examined the evidence, and he could not deny there was a problem. Authorities questioned that perhaps Dr. Shipman had devised a kind of fantasy plan by which he could get Ms. Grundy's money and run away and stop being a doctor. She was his last victim and his motive seemed to be different than all of his other victims.

Kathleen Grundy's body was exhumed and a post-mortem autopsy revealed that she had died of a morphine overdose administered within three hours of her death. Precisely within the time frame of when Dr. Shipman had been to her cottage.

In early August a taxi driver by the name of John Shaw from Hyde, also contacted the police. He told the police that he suspected Dr. Shipman of being involved in something, because he had driven the doctor to 21 of the houses where the patients died shortly after the doctor visited them.

Shipman's home was raided, yielding all of his medical records and an odd collection of jewelry, an old typewriter which proved to be the instrument upon which Grundy's forged will had been produced.

It was immediately apparent to the police from the medical records seized that the case would extend further than the single death in question and priority was given to those deaths it would be most productive to investigate. Namely victims who had not been cremated, and had died following a home visit from Dr. Shipman.

Shipman had urged a large number of his families to cremate their relatives. There was no further investigation of those deaths, even in instances when these relatives had died of causes previously unknown to the families.

In situations where they did raise questions Shipman would provide computerized medical notes that corroborated the death certificate. Police later established that Shipman would in most cases alter these medical notes directly after killing the patient to ensure that his account matched the historical records.

The historical records Shipman had failed to grasp was that each alteration of records would be time stamped by the computer. Leading police to ascertain exactly which records had been altered.

Following extreme investigations which includes numerous exhumations and autopsies the police charged Shipman with fifteen counts of murder. Harold Frederick Shipman was arrested on September 7, 1998 and charged with fifteen individual counts of murder and one count of forgery. His trial was to begin on October 5, 1999.

The prosecutor asserted that Shipman had killed fifteen patients because he enjoyed exercising control over life and death. They dismissed any claims that he had been acting compassionately, as none of the victims were suffering a terminal illness.

Angela Woodruff, Kathleen Grundy's daughter appeared as the first witness. Her forthright manner and account of her unrelenting determination to get to the truth impressed the jury, and attempts by Shipman's defense to undermine her were largely unsuccessful.

Next the government pathologist led the court through the gruesome post mortem findings where morphine toxicity was the cause of death in most cases. He had injected each patient with diamorphine a pharmaceutical form of heroin.

Other doctors and nurses who worked with him stated that Dr. Shipman never seemed nervous or distraught. They would have never guessed that he had been killing his patients. Apparently, he would kill his victims and then he carried on as if nothing ever happened. One nurse testified that she often worked alone with Dr. Shipman and she never suspected any unusual behavior at all, and she had worked with him for many years.

It was soon discovered that Shipman had concealed large masses of diamorphine. After months of research it was uncovered that he had secretly obtained more than 24,000 milligrams of diamorphine illicitly between 1992 and 1998. He misappropriated enough to kill at least 720 patients.

The large amounts of stolen diamorphine led to a much larger investigation. It was discovered that Dr. Shipman had killed as many as 215 to possibly 260 patients by injecting them with lethal doses of painkillers. He would kill his patients and then attribute the death to natural causes.

The motives behind the killings have remained unclear. Some believed that he was angry about the death of his mother. Others thought he was practicing euthanasia and eliminating the older people as he thought they were a burden on the health care system. Many of the authorities thought that he derived pleasure from the fact that as a doctor he had the power to grant someone either life or death, and killing was a means to express his power.

The coroner John Pollard stated that he believed that Shipman derived pleasure from watching his patients die. He said, "Dr. shipman enjoyed viewing the process of dying and he liked the feeling of power of giving someone life or death. Financial gain didn't seem like one of the main motives at that time."

A team of psychological and psychiatric experts failed to come up with anything concrete of why Shipman killed his patients. They pondered motive, personal relationships with patients, aggression, dishonesty, but nothing explained his actions. The judge in the case, Dame Janet Smith said, "without motive or rational or conscience explanation for committing a crime …I think his crimes were without motive."

Primrose Shipman, Dr. Shipman's wife always stood by his side. She told authorities that she had never suspected her husband of any wrong doings. He was gone a lot, but she knew he was dedicated to his work. As far as the authorities could tell, his four children also stood by him.

On January 31, 2000 a jury found Dr. Harold Frederick Shipman guilty of killing fifteen patients under his care. He was sentenced to life imprisonment with the recommendation that he never be released. He is the only British doctor to have ever been found guilty of murdering his patients. Although, other doctors have been acquitted of similar crimes.

Dr. Harold Frederick Shipman continuously denied his guilt, disputing all of the scientific evidence against him. A senior West Yorkshire detective by the name of Chris Gregg was selected to lead the investigation into 22 of the West Yorkshire deaths. As he got deeper into the investigation, he discovered that Dr. Shipman had been involved in as many as 215 to 260 patients. After further checking they discovered that as many as 459 people had actually died under Dr. Shipman's care from 1971 to 1998.

In March of 2002 I flew to England to write a documented article on Dr. Harold Shipman, the doctor known as Doctor Death. For this interview I talked with several of the people who had been directly involved in his case. The first person I interviewed was Angela Woodruff, the daughter of Kathleen Grundy. Kathleen Grundy was the last known person to have been killed by Dr. Shipman. I then interviewed three of Dr. Shipman's colleagues, Detective Superintendent Postles of the local police department and John Shaw the taxi driver.

I had a lengthy interview with the coroner John Pollard and the government pathologists that led the court through the post-mortem findings. I also interviewed eight of the family members involved in the original investigations, and the senior West Yorkshire detective Chris Gregg who discovered the lengthy list of possible killings long after the sentencing was completed. Dr. Shipman's wife, Primrose Shipman refused to meet with me. I was only allowed these private interviews because the doctor's trial had been over for quite some time and sentencing was completed.

I met with Dr. Harold Shipman himself on March 16, 2002. It was only fair to the doctor that I meet with him in person after meeting with so many of the other people involved in the trial.

Dr. Shipman was not at all as I had expected. If I didn't know better, I would have never believed this man to be a killer. Although, he was shackled he appeared confident, intelligent and not the least bit remorseful for anything that he had done. In fact, he kind of ridiculed the family members that had testified against him. During our interview he never confessed, denied his guilt or acted upset about the way his life had gone.

Much of the arrogance that the other people had warned me about was still very apparent. As the doctor talked, I sat and studied his behavior. I have done many interviews all across the globe, but this man was a very difficult person to analyze. Nevertheless, I got my personal interview, and that was really all that I could expect, but I left that day feeling quite confused. I could not understand how someone could kill so many helpless people, and yet act so indifferent about it.

Less than two years after I visited Dr. Harold Frederick Shipman in the Wakefield Prison, he hung himself from the window bars of his cell using his own bedsheets. He died on January 13, 2004, the day before his fifty-eighth birthday.

His suicide divided the National newspapers with some calling him a 'cold coward' and others disappointed because he had never given the families any answers. Many were upset at the prison system for allowing this to happen in the first place. Some newspapers even celebrated with headlines saying 'Ship, Ship hooray."

Shipman's motive for suicide was never established though he often told his probation officer he was distressed.

When Shipman was arrested in 1998, they had found over 10,000 units of jewelry hidden in his garage. It later came to light that Shipman might have stolen jewelry from many of his victims.

A memorial garden to Shipman's victims called the 'Garden of Tranquility' opened in Hyde Park on July 30, 2005. Families of the victims of Dr. Shipman will be seeking compensation for the loss of their relatives for many years.

After my return from England I was haunted for months about my interview with Dr. Shipman. I couldn't believe that I had actually sat and talked with someone who thought that he had the right to decide when his patients lived or died. He had absolutely no regard for human life. He was their family doctor, and they trusted him, but at his time of choosing he just gave them an injection and put them to sleep.

Dr. Shipman is probably the worst killer of all time, because he personally knew every one of the people that he killed. As far as anyone could analyze, he wasn't angry, jealous or upset with any of the patients he killed, and he knew all of them very well. Many of them he had treated for years. Oftentimes, he also knew all of their family members. He must have known that after his patient had died the families would be grieving and heart-broken, and his heartless actions would separate his patient from their families forever, yet he didn't seem to care.

Harold Shipman looked each patient directly in the eyes, and injected them with his poison, then watched them sit back and silently die. I shudder to think that a sane person could really do this.

My thoughts always return to my own family when I write an article that is very disturbing like this one. I am now a grandfather, with adult children of my own. Our oldest son, Nick is a Nazarene minister and he is married to our beautiful daughter-in-law Mary. They live in Boise with their two children, Connie and Roger. Next, we have Mary Ellen and her husband Richard and they have five children, Diane, Ruth, Tammy, Teddi and Byron.

We also helped raise my brother's three children, Holly, Lou, and Douglas. My brother's children are several years older than our kids, so of course, they are all grown and out on their own.

Sarah and I still have our two youngest children living at home. Our daughter Carolyn is a High School cheerleader, and our youngest son Ronald plays in the school's marching band.

One of the reasons that Dr. Shipman's story troubled me so much is not only because of my own family, but because it had only been a short time since our country had experienced 9/11. It was so difficult for me to accept the fact that people hated other people enough to actually calculate their murders.

After my private interview with Dr. Shipman, I couldn't help wondering what it would have been like to sit down for an interview with the hijackers before the attack of the World Trade Center.

Would they too have felt superior? Would they in some inexplicable way try to persuade me that what they were planning was right. Would they try to convince me that it was all right to kill thousands of innocent people because they were all just infidels, and they did not have the same beliefs or objectives as the terrorists? I am deeply saddened at the absolute disregard for life that all of these killers have for their innocent victims.

In Dr. Shipman's case he knew his victims personally. He had talked with them, he had cared for them, often times he made them healthy when they were sick, and then when they were in good health…he quietly injected them and put them to sleep.

Many times, after my return from interviewing Dr. Shipman, I had sincerely wished that I had never gone to England to do the interview. I was tormented by the reality that someone could actually find pleasure in injecting a healthy person with diamorphine, and putting them to sleep like a veterinarian would euthanize a sick animal.

A short time after my interview with Dr. Shipman I was asked to write an article about the tremendous advances of modern medicine taking place in the twenty-first Century. After the bizarre story about Dr. Shipman I was more than delighted to shift my energies to something more upbeat and inspiring.

***

Throughout history medical science has become capable of so many spectacular feats. It was absolutely amazing to me to be able to do studies on the eleven most challenging surgeries of the past century.

During this research I was able to interview several of the top surgeons of our country. These brilliant doctors appear to have super-human skills. I talked with specialists that do repair surgeries that are nothing short of miracles. On several different occasions, I was allowed to sit in the observation booth, "the Dome", to actually witness the remarkable surgery taking place before me.

The first surgery that I observed was called a **Thoracic Aortic Dissection Repair**. It is an emergency surgery to fix a tear in the deepest layer of the human heart. It is often the reason for heart failure, stroke, or even a rupture of the aorta.

Next, I viewed a **Bladder Cystectomy**. It is for patients with bladder cancer and it involves removing a part of the urinary bladder, sometimes the entire bladder.

One of the most difficult surgeries that I was told about was a **Septic Myectomy**. This is a surgery to unclog the congealed muscles of the heart. The most challenging part of this surgery is that it needs to be performed on a motionless heart.

I was surprised to discover that one of the most problematic surgeries to perform is the **Bariatric Surgery/Gastric Bypass**. This is a surgery for weight loss and for reducing the size of the stomach. The procedure is a very challenging surgery since the internal organs are hard to separate, and in most cases, they have a layer of slippery fat surrounding them. One of the reasons there is a higher risk for complications during this surgery is the difficulties that occur from the anesthesia. The dosage needs to be a higher dose because it is easily absorbed by the fat, this makes the dosage very hard to regulate.

Spinal Osteomyelitis Surgery is an infection of the vertebrae in the spine. Surgery of the spine is very dangerous because there are extreme risks of being fully or partially paralyzed. The doctors strongly encourage other treatments before suggesting surgery.

One of the most fascinating surgeries that I wrote about was the doctors who separated **Conjoined Twins**. This surgery is a true miracle of life and medicine. It requires a varied set of specialists to carry out the separation. The surgery requires several specialists in the surgery room at the same time. A neurosurgeon for the brain, and an orthopedics/plastic surgeon for the hands and legs.

This was truly the greatest surgery that I observed. This miraculous procedure actually brought tears to my eyes. To think that this team of brilliant doctors could successfully separate conjoined children, and make them two separate individuals that are healthy and can live apart. I was in awe.

Coronary Revascularization is the surgery to restore the flow of blood to the heart. The procedure uses artery or vein grafts from another part of the patient's body to make new connections.

A Craniectomy is an invasive surgery that requires a parting of the skull to inspect the brain. It is one of the riskiest surgeries because the surgeon must drill through a portion of the skull to reach the brain. It is one of the most dangerous surgeries because there is a high chance of a stroke, seizures, or fluid leakage, and swelling of the brain.

Surgical Ventricular Restoration is the surgery used to restore the heart to its regular shape and size after an attack. The procedure is complex and it is very high risk because the procedure is done to fix congestive heart failure after an attack and to make it function again. The patient is put on a heart-lung machine while the surgeon is dealing with this precise part of the body.

Esophagectomy is the removal and reconstruction of the esophagus. It is the reconstruction of the region between the stomach and the esophagus.

Pancreatectomy is the surgical removal of the pancreas. It has been reported and documented that there has been a numerous amount of complications with this surgery. Several patients have reported post-operative bleeding, delayed gastric erupting and internal anastomotic leaking.

While flying home on the plane after days of interviews with the surgeons, I had a lot of time to think. Over the past few days I had learned so much about the complicated surgeries that these remarkable doctors perform, and I realized that doctors all over the world, are doing the exact same surgeries, and they too are saving lives each and every day.

My mind was on over-load, but I felt so elated because I was allowed to actually observe the miracles that these doctors perform. I just couldn't help but praise the Lord for the great wonders of our time. Before these surgeons mastered the skill to achieve these miraculous surgeries; people just died. To think that a normal human being had been granted such wisdom and the unique ability to renew the life of patients that they really don't even know.

I covered my face with both of my hands, and shook my head to try to clear my confusion. I thought to myself, "It is so perplexing to me that we have these miraculous doctors that save lives, and change our world, and we have advanced so far in saving lives. Yet, we also have people like Dr. Shipman and the terrorists of 9/11 who think nothing of eradicating as many people as possible. How can a world with so much good, be filled with so much hatred, and such a craving for power? I fear for the future generations."

I casually glanced around the plane, and for the first time in all the years that I have flown, I felt afraid. "Who are these people?" I thought to myself. "Is that dark-bearded man staring out the window a terrorist? Are the two nervous looking athletes in the next seat, actually killers? Is the lady with the covering over her head, a suicide bomber? For the first time since I came on the plane, I realized very few of the people are smiling, talking or paying attention to anyone around them. How many of them are filled with hate for Christians, white people or the wealthy? Do they resent America like so many people that we read about in all of the newspapers? Do they burn our flag? Do they feel they have the right to live in America, and disrespect our police, our military and our government?"

I shook my head to clear it and I thought, "I have always looked at people, and tried to accept them the way they are, but I have seen and heard too much in the past few years. As I have gotten older, I now know that we can no longer tell the good guys from the bad."

My heart sank as I considered my own family, "My children and my grandchildren are forced to live in a dangerous new universe. We are no longer in a world where young children can play in the park alone, or walk to the corner grocery store, or even go to the restroom without an adult. Since all of the rules about gender have changed, both men and women can use any bathroom, making it unsafe for our children."

I shook my head and thought to myself, "It is so hard for me to understand all of the discontent and changes that have taken place. Yet, I see it daily, in government politics, in corporations, in the media, in other cultures, in our churches, in friendships, in schools, and even in our families. Democrats, Republicans, Christians, Atheists, Muslins, Mormons, Catholics, Jews." I shook my head back and forth in disbelief, then ran my fingers through my hair, and sighed, "I am ready to be home," I silently said to myself.

Eleven

Cloning

A short time after I finished my article about the surgeons, I was asked to work on a cloning project. I knew the research would be fairly simple, and quite interesting, so I started working on it right away.

Cloning is the process of producing genetically identical individuals or organism either naturally or artificially. Human cloning is the creation of genetically identical copy of an existing or previously existing human being or growing cloned tissue from that individual.

The first mammal to be cloned from an adult somatic cell, using the process of nuclear transfer was a female domestic sheep named Dolly. She was born on July 5, 1996 in Scotland, United Kingdom. Dolly was named after the well-known singer, Dolly Parton. When she was first born, she was so perfect that she was expected to live for eleven or twelve years, the normal lifespan of a domestic sheep. Yet, as healthy as she first appeared, problems started to occur as she aged. At around six years old she began developing liver disease and severe arthritis.

In her lifetime, she delivered six healthy babies, first Bonnie, then twins Sally and Rosie, then triplets Lucy, Darcy and Cotton. With each offspring Dolly's arthritis continued to get worse. At just under seven years old, Dolly was euthanized on February 14, 2003. She had severe liver disease and crippling arthritis. Her remains are on display in the National Museum of Scotland.

Other mammal cloning had been attempted by Steen Willadsen in 1984. Willadsen graduated from the Royal Veterinary College, and the cloning was done from early embryonic cells, while Dolly was cloned from an adult cell.

Two sheep Megan and Morag were sheep that were cloned from differentiated embryonic cells in 1995. Yet, Dolly proved to be the first clone created as a genetically identical copy.

The first hybrid human clone was created in November 1998 by advanced cell technology. It was created using SCNT (somatic cell nuclear transfer), a nucleus was taken from a man's leg cell, and inserted into a cow's egg from which the nucleus had been removed. A hybrid cell was cultured and developed into an embryo, but the embryo was destroyed twelve days later.

Hans Spemann was a German embryologist who was awarded a Nobel Prize in Physiology medicine in 1935 for his discovery of the effect now known as embryonic induction. An influence exercised by various parts of the embryo, that directs the development of groups of cells into a clone is a group of identical cells that share a common ancestry, meaning they are derived from the same cell. Clonality is the fact or condition of being genetically identical as a parent, siblings or other biological sources. Clonality is a state of proliferation determined by the cells or origin daughter cells arising from multiple cells.

A cloning vector is a small piece of DNA taken from a plasmid, or the cell of a higher organism, that can be stably maintained in an organism, and into which a foreign DNA fragment can be inserted for cloning purposes. Dolly used the process of nuclear transfer.

Clonality is important in treating diseases and understanding its physiopathology. Clonality is the ability to be cloned. The use of cloning techniques was created for perfectly matched tissues that would someday cure ailments ranging from diabetes to Parkinson disease. Nonetheless, the research has been an ethical debate, tainted with fraud in recent years.

In 1996 a donor cell from the body tissue such as skin is fused with an unfertilized egg from which the nucleus has been removed. The egg "reprograms" the DNA in the donor cell to an embryonic state and divides until it has reached the early blastocyst stage. The cells are then harvested and cultured to create a stable cell line that is genetically matched to the donor and that can become almost any cell type in the human body.

Many scientists have tried to create human SCNT cell lines: none had succeeded until now. Most infamously, Woo Suk Hwang of Seoul National University in South Korea used hundreds of human eggs to report two successes in 2004 and 2005. Both turned out to be unsuccessful. Other researchers made some headway.

Some of the specialists working on the project found the cells had abnormal numbers of chromosomes, limiting their use. The researchers tested them in various combinations in more than 1,000 monkey eggs before moving on to human cells. They finally made the right improvements. Researchers have used the cloning method that produced Dolly the sheep to create two healthy monkeys, genetically identical long-tailed macaques. They are the first nonhuman primates every born. The two timid animals are named Zhong Zhong and Hua Hua, a Mandarin term that means Chinese nation and people.

Scientists feel that successfully cloning monkeys could lead to treating many diseases, but many people feel that this is just one step closer to cloning humans. It is a significant step in developing the cells that could be used in regenerative medicine.

The research team was led by scientists at the Oregon Health and Science University, who used a similar technique as the one successful with Dolly the Sheep.

The process relies on human reproductive eggs that have been donated by female volunteers, which have not been fertilized. The unfertilized eggs used in the study were donated by several young women recruited through a university program. They were paid between $3,000 and up to $7,000 in compensation. The researchers behind the new work say the fact the donor cells were unfertilized should help avoid ongoing controversy over previous research involving the destruction of fertilized embryos which are able to grow into full human beings if left up to nature.

Another company that was formed in 1997 is called the Clonaid Company. The Clonaid Company was organized by the Raelian cult, and it has announced that they have completed the first cloned baby. The president of the company Brigette Boisselier said that the baby was born in the Bahamas, but there was no proof or exact confirmation of the cloned birth.

Boisselier said, "The healthy baby was a girl named Eve. Her mother was a thirty-one-year-old American woman whose partner is infertile. The baby was delivered by Caesarian section, weighing seven pounds." Boisselier says you can easily prove that the baby is a clone of another person by showing that the DNA is identical. The Raelian cult strongly believes that many people are clones of aliens.

Many scientists are skeptical of Boisselier's claim. Specialists from Melbourne, Australia say, "I do not believe the company Clonaid has the necessary expertise to really clone a person. They have been proven wrong in the past."

Opponents of human cloning point to the high rate of miscarriages of animal fetuses, and to the high rate of defects in live births. Boisselier claimed that they have such a large number of female cult members that are willing to be surrogate mothers; that increases their chances for success.

A few year ago, Barbara Streisand revealed to 'Variety Magazine' that she had her dog cloned for $50,000, many people learned for the first time that copying pets and other animals is a real business.

Trying to clone humans is irresponsible and it ignores the over-whelming scientific evidence that has been collected. A U.S. based fertility scientist told the U.S. congress that five groups of scientists were rushing to be the first to produce the first cloned human baby.

Reproductive cloning-creating a baby rather than a cloned embryo is illegal in many countries. Also, the possibility of human cloning has raised controversies. Reproductive cloning would involve making an entire cloned human, instead of just specific cells or tissue.

The ethics of cloning refers to a variety of ethical positions regarding the practice and possibilities of cloning, especially human cloning. Many of the views are religious, and the questions raised by cloning are faced by secular perspectives as well. Human therapeutic and reproductive cloning are not commonly used. Animals are currently cloned in laboratories and in livestock production.

Advocates support development of therapeutic cloning in order to generate tissue and whole organs to treat patients. They also, believe that parents that cannot otherwise procreate should have access to the technology. Opposition to therapeutic cloning mainly centers around the status of embryonic stem cells, which has connections with the abortion debate.

Some opponents of reproductive cloning have concerns that the technology is not developed enough to be safe. Also, religious groups are divided, with some opposing the technology as usurping God's role in creation and to the extent embryos are used, destroying a human life. Yet, others support therapeutic cloning's potential life-saving benefits.

In conclusion, by the year 2015 seventy countries have completely banned human cloning.

Twelve

Fake News

During my lifetime, I have seen the world take on so many unexpected changes. I started my writing career at the age of nine years old when I first wrote about the lady that lived next door. From that time on, I knew I wanted to be a journalist. As a young person, I won numerous awards for creative writing. I started out writing small local newspaper articles, and continually proceeded on from there.

I took various writing courses when I was younger. I started with English literature, creative writing, and of course several quick journalism classes, but the main key to my success was my ability to work independently, and to keep myself focused.

I was fortunate enough to be able to succeed on my accrued accomplishments until one day I found myself interviewing people all over the world. One editorial led to another. I realize that my success came at a very unique time in history. Because the young people of today must take several years of journalism courses before they can even get their foot in the door of most companies. It takes them a long time to accomplish what I have been blessed to do all of my lifetime.

The drastic changes that I have seen taking place in the journalism realm is almost too incomprehensible for me to accept. It deeply troubles me to stand in a large conference room with other reporters and listen to a spokesperson talk, only to have many of the journalists standing with me misrepresent the words that were said by the speaker. It is like none of us hear the same thing. It almost seems as if some of the other reporters are told what to say or what to write about ahead of time; long before the speaker even begins to speak.

I've watched as other journalist began shouting accusations at the person speaking, even before they have finished with what they are saying. Then they get upset and storm out of the conference room, and take half the people in the room with them. They act like small children that are throwing a tantrum because they do not get their way. The few people left, like me, just stand in awe and wonder what was said that was so upsetting. I have witnessed this behavior time and time again in the past few years.

The disrespect for other people is probably the worst part of everything that is taking place. They outshout each other, and they holler at the person speaking as if they are not even worth talking to.

We all started out in our careers as journalist, always informing the public on what we had seen or heard. Only stating the facts, not our opinions. Then we became reporters, only reporting the facts, keeping our opinions to ourselves. Today many of us have become activists, reporting things the way we want the public to see things rather than the way it truly is.

It puzzles me that certain publications write the identical articles as their sister stations. They report word for word as their associated stations report. It sounds more like propaganda, than news. It is as if one main source is controlling every one of the writers on many of the major networks. Journalism didn't used to be this way. For most of my career being a journalist was an honor, something that I was very proud of, but news no longer seems to be news. Our job used to be to let people know the truth about the things that were happening in our world, but recently the media seems to be spinning things around to create the perceptions that they want the people to believe.

As my fellow reporters and I stand together in a large auditorium, we all hear exactly the same thing. Yet, they will later report things completely different than what had actually been said. It is frightening to me, because I know that a scathing article can slant or even completely change the views of the readers and listeners.

It truly saddens me because journalism has almost become a joke. Many of the journalist and news reporters that had once been held in high esteem are now often distorting the truth and being believed because they had always proven trustworthy in the past. They constantly embellished the facts just to sensationalize their stories.

One reporter commented, "If it bleeds, it leads." Many writers would do anything to destroy someone's reputation, credibility, and influence. It is as if their own integrity is totally abandoned by causing all of the commotion when they publish things that are half-truth or completely fabricated. They knowingly print articles just to confuse their readers, and to plant doubt, and to get everyone arguing about things.

Now that I am older, I can stand back and see the vicious competition taking place amongst all of the news reporters. It is truly disheartening because many people honestly seem like they hate each other, and they will say and do anything to try to convince everyone around them to believe the same way they believe. It is worse now than I have ever seen in my lifetime.

My entire life I have been taught to look for the good in people, and believe me after some of the bizarre interviews that I have done, that has not always been easy. It frightens me because in today's world, I watch the hatred and dishonesty spiraling out of control. So many of my fellow news reporters thrive on hostility towards certain leading politicians, and they will try their hardest to destroy them at all cost. Even if they ruin their own reputations in the process. So many people in this world seem so angry, and they argue about everything.

Another strange narrative that some of the television news casters are starting to do, is to choose one small piece out of an interview, and show it over and over again. They disregard the rest of the feature, and just show the small clip that they want the public to see.

They know that just one small clip taken out of context can oftentimes completely change the public's opinion of the person being interviewed. This is happening a lot in political interviews. The interviewer doesn't like the person they are forced to interview, and they don't care who knows it. They ask discriminatory, insulting questions; slanderous questions that they would never ask a person that they liked or admired.

It is genuinely tragic because the journalists can completely sway the feelings of the audience by cropping certain parts out of the interview. It can really be confusing, because the public knows that they can see the interview with their own eyes, yet they are not aware of everything that had been said, because so many things had been edited out.

To me, this is dishonesty, and it is embarrassing to witness. I have called other reporters on this on several different occasions, but they just shrug their shoulders and reply, "The jerk deserves it."

I hate to see journalism, my chosen career, destroyed this way. A seasoned reporter knows that he can shift the opinion of his viewers, just by what is being said. He can make the person that is being interviewed look angry, weak or corrupt just by showing a partial conversation.

The term Fake News has become very popular in the past few elections. It is so confusing, even for an older journalist like me. Because a good writer can easily convince the public that what they are writing about is the absolute truth; even if it is twisted or fabricated. Unlike advertisements many people accept every news article to be true unless proven otherwise. They feel the newscasters can't report it, if isn't the truth.

Being the first network to get a breaking news story out has become much more important than waiting to secure the true facts. Many newspapers and television news reports have started doing small retractions, stating that the article that they published wasn't entirely true, but most people never see the retraction. Statistics show that the public usually believes what was first reported. Readers trust that the story must be true, because they trust the station reporting it.

It is becoming much easier for news reporters and television announcers to tell half-truths when they are broadcasting the news. They just say what the network tells them to say, and the reporters are rarely held accountable.

They want to keep their jobs, so they just report on what they are told to report. They never even question the story's validity. Yet, recently some of the top ranked newscasters in the industry have lost their jobs because of blindly peddling fake news. Many of the highest paid reporters in the country have been accused of arrogance, sexual misconduct, and misleading news reports.

For some reason they see themselves as untouchable and irreplaceable. I've stood right next to them two minutes before they go live, and they say slanderous things about the people they are reporting about. For some reason the reporters feel they are far superior to the people they are speaking about. They think the viewers will believe anything they tell them. It is inconceivable to me how disgraceful some of the most well-known newscaster have become.

When they go live their whole demeanor changes, and they become the kind, trustworthy reporter that the people expect them to be. They are so smug that they think they can say and do anything that they want to, because they are so popular, so important, and so high above everyone else that they can't be touched.

Yet in recent months, many of the top news reporters have actually been forced to apologize to their viewers for the misleading reports that they have given, then to their overwhelming surprise, they are quietly replaced in their job.

Much of the false information is distributed by social media, but sometimes it also, seeps through the mainstream media. Fake news is written and published with the intent to mislead in order to damage an agency, entity or a certain person. It is often used to gain financial or political fame. The media has learned that sensationalizing, being dishonest or outright fabricating a headline will increase their popularity and improve their ratings. It also, attracts users and benefits the advertisers.

A lot of the confusion with the media started after the development of the internet, the use of Facebook, Twitter and Google. The general populace then had many other resources to get their information rather than just their regular News outlets.

Fake news undermines the serious media coverage and makes it more difficult for significant news stories to be recognized. Fake news is often used to refer to fabricated news on social media. Fake news has no basis for fact, but it is presented as being accurate.

The producer of CBS 60 Minutes said, "My show considers fake news to be stories that are probably false, but they have enormous traction and popularity. They are consumed by millions. These stories can be found not only in politics, but also in numerous things such as stock values and nutrition."

Propaganda can be fake news. Some commentators say fake news is just satire, with no goal to do harm to anyone. They say it has no intention of deceiving or confusing. When genuine content is used with false information, it is called misleading. Yet, with fabricated content, when they know that it is 100% false, it truly is designed to divide and do harm. Also, when genuine content is used with false information and is manipulated to deceive as with a doctored photograph the public begins to question every report. All of this has destroyed the public's trust in the news media. In fact, a Gallup Confidence poll found that only about 20% Americans have confidence in truth in television, and approximately 23% of the public has confidence in newspaper reports.

Although, fake news is nothing new. It goes all the way back to the 13th century B.C. when Rameses the Great spread lies portraying The Battle of Kadesh as a strong victory for the Egyptians and the Hittites when actually it was proven to be a stalemate.

During the first century B.C. Octavian ran a campaign of misinformation against his rival Mark Antony portraying Antony as a drunkard, a womanizer, and a mere puppet of the Egyptian queen, Cleopatra VII.

He even published a document purporting to be Marc Antony's will which claimed Marc Antony wished to be entombed in the Mausoleum of the Ptolemaic Pharaohs. Although, the document was forged it invoked outrage from the Roman populace.

Marc Antony ultimately killed himself after his defeat in the Battle of Actium. He killed himself after hearing false rumors propagated by Cleopatra herself, claiming that she had committed suicide.

Another instance of fake news was during the second and third centuries A.D. False rumors were spread about Christians claiming that they engage in cannibalism and incest.

In 1945 a fake news story claimed that the Jewish Community had murdered a 2 ½ year old Christian infant. The story resulted in all of the Jews being arrested and tortured. Fifteen of them were burned at the stake. Pope Sixtus IV himself attempted to stamp out the story, but it had already spread beyond anyone's control.

In the twenty-first century fake news became widespread as well as the usage of the term. The beginning of the internet in the nineties was meant to allow access to information, but over time the internet became a source of unwanted, untruthful and misleading information that can be made up by anyone. It is also called the satirical news, whose purpose is not to mislead, but rather to inform viewers and share humorous commentary about real news and the mainstream media. Sadly, the news reports are now much like the late-night stand-up comedians, who make their living ridiculing and slandering other people.

The tragedy in all of this confusion is the public is smarter than the reporters give them credit for. Most people can see through the nonsense and they are choosing to distrust any media.

The fake news is often intended to increase the financial profits of news outlets. A former CEO of one of the fake news media conglomerates said, "At one time my company employed 20 to 25 writers and made 10 to 30 thousand dollars in advertising a week."

He began his career in journalism as a magazine salesman before working as a freelance writer. He said, "I entered the fake news industry to prove to myself and others just how rapidly fake news can spread."

I discovered that the top 20 fake news stories about the 2016 U.S. Presidential election received more attention on Facebook than the top 20 election stories from the top media outlets. Facebook has been searching for ways to flag fake news reports, but it is difficult to distinguish real news from fake news.

Fake news is often used to refer to fabricated news. Social media or fake news websites have no basis for fact, but is presented as being accurate.

There are approximately seven different fake news organizations operating all the time. They employ hundreds of teenagers that rapidly produce and plagiarize sensational stories for a number of different US based companies and parties.

A certain writer with the last name of Horner was behind several widespread hoaxes. He stated that many of his hoaxes were to make the people on the Donald Trump campaign look foolish. He said that he finally stopped because he had written so many slanderous articles that had actually helped the Trump campaign rather than hurt it. Mr. Horner decided that the Trump Bible thumpers were going to vote for Trump no matter what he said.

After creating several different fake news articles Horner told reporters the importance of fact checking. He said that he wrote fake news solely to be misleading. Horner said that he wrote fake news just to be writing fake news. He said that there was no purpose, no satire, nothing clever, he was just trying to make Trump supporters look like idiots for sharing his stories. The Huffington Post called Mr. Horner a "Performance Artist." He has also been called a "Hoax Artists" by outlets like the Associated Press, and Chicago Tribune.

A 2016 study by researchers from Princeton University, Dartmouth College and the University of Exeter has examined the consumption of fake news during the 2016 U.S. presidential campaign. The findings showed Trump supporters and older Americans over 60 were more likely to consume fake news. Facebook was the "gateway" website when these fake news stories were spread.

Over the past few Presidential elections people have grown more and more apprehensive towards the government. It seems that if their candidate does not win the election, they spend the next several years bad-mouthing the other candidate, and refusing to accept them as the new President.

When I witness the confusion being published in so many of the news outlets, I am somewhat ashamed by the things that are taking place. Even if the fabricated and oftentimes slanderous material that is being written has nothing to do with me, I am still a recognized journalist, and I am joined together with the other journalists because of my credentials, and I am truly embarrassed.

Many of the protestors are professional protestors, they are essentially hired and paid to march for some certain cause. The tragedy about all of the hired protestors is that many of the marchers don't even care about the cause that they are shouting about. They don't have regular jobs, and they are just doing what they were hired to do, but to the general public it appears that hundreds of marchers are truly upset about the cause they are marching for. These hired protestors seem to be effective, because they continually keep the public in constant turmoil.

I believe in freedom of speech, but over the past few years freedom of speech means freedom to protests, march, obstruct justice, slander people, and harm whoever gets in the way. It seems that people are protesting something every day of the week, and they appear to get much more attention than the everyday working people who actually support the country.

We live in a new era. It is a time of protesting and ridicule. People seem to be angry about everything, and they don't hesitate to let their opinion be known. They are just outraged about one thing after another, and they insist that their voices be heard. Once again, one of the main ways that they express their opinion is by marching in masses.

One of the first peaceful assemblies that started the marches was on August 28, 1963. Approximately 250,000 people participated in the civil rights march in Washington DC when Martin Luther King Jr. delivered his famous, "I have a dream" speech.

On the fifteenth of November 1969, between 500,000 to 600,000 people demonstrated in Washington DC because they were angry about the war in Vietnam.

The Solidarity Day march in September 1981 was a rally in response to President Ronald Reagan's decision to fire 12,000 air traffic controllers who went on strike and demanded a wage increase and safer working conditions.

In the year 1982 over a million people from around the world filled Central Park to protest Nuclear energy.

On October 11, 1987 the second national march was held in Washington DC for Lesbians and Gay rights. The march was also known as the "Great March." The march called for federal money for Aids research and treatment, as well as an end to discrimination against the LGBT people. Then again on April 25, 1993 they marched for Lesbians, Gay and Bi-people and for equal rights and liberation.

October 16, 1995 was the day of the Million Man march in Washington DC. It took place with the aim to unite the Black community. Approximately, 400,000 to up to one million people marched that day.

Two years later on October 25, 1997 in Philadelphia, Pennsylvania almost two million people marched in the pouring rain to unite the Black women. It was a peaceful march that included prayer, musical performances and speakers.

In 2003 there were protest held against the Iraq War. It was estimated that there were about 600 cities across the world where people protested. At least 500,000 people marched in American cities.

On April 25, 2004 the march for women's lives was held. It was said to be one the largest pro-choice protest in American history with 500,000 to one and a half million marchers.

It seems that some group is protesting something every week or so, but very few have gotten violent. One of the most troublesome was on February 8, 2017, shortly after President Trump was inaugurated, there was a Women's March in Washington DC. They wore obscene hats on their heads and carried vulgar signs.

People could never say the things about their President in other countries, the way Americans talk about the President of the United States. All of the jokes, slander and animosity towards people in the government have been vicious, hateful and completely disrespectful. Fake news has proven to be the enemy of truth; therefore, it is the enemy of the people.

Thirteen

How Did We get Here?

Throughout my career I have written over 28,000 magazine and newspaper articles. I have published fourteen books, seventy-two short stories, and thirty-eight journals. During my lengthy career I have interviewed Presidents, world dignitaries, rock stars, killers, evangelists, doctors, policeman, billionaires, and congressmen. I have talked with scientists, astronauts, drug dealers, college students, movie stars, mayors, CEO's, and other journalists. I have also interviewed school teachers, trash collectors, and union workers who were not allowed to cross the picket lines. I have spent time with homeless people on the streets, as well as those who live in sanctuary cities, or in their cars.

My wife Sarah and I have been overseas on several different occasions, and we have journeyed to 42 of the 50 states, in America. Throughout my lifetime I have flown over 150,000 miles, and I have visited hundreds of wonderful destinations throughout the world.

I've taught a variety of contemporary writing courses, and have been involved in a number of job evaluation projects for several large corporations.

This astonishing career has taken me to places that I could only dream of going. I have been the honored speaker at seminars, conferences and conventions throughout the world. All of my life I have loved the variety that my writing has given to me. This has truly been a magnificent profession.

Yet, it is sometimes overwhelming for me to think about how drastically journalism has changed since the beginning of my career. The innocence, respectability, and truth has so often been pushed aside by many journalists and been replaced by the greed of money, popularity, and success.

I have always taken my writing seriously. It saddens me to think that I could mislead my readers by putting in my opinion and trying to change their minds so that they think the way I want them to think.

Now that I am older, and have lived a full life, I realize that my writing is a unique gift that was given to me from God. The love of writing that I discovered at nine years old, has remained with me throughout my entire lifetime.

One thing that I have discovered after doing hundreds of personal interviews throughout the years, is that you should never act afraid when interviewing certain people. I learned not to change the expression on my face as I talk with someone. It is oftentimes difficult for me not to over-react to what I am being told. No matter how disturbing or frightened I may feel by what is being said, I try to remain calm. Oftentimes, my heart is rapidly beating, and I can scarcely catch my breath. I am seriously petrified, but I know I must just wait and listen, even though I feel like running.

Sometimes, even the location where the interview is taking place has made me uncomfortable, but I just desperately pray and try to remain calm and get through the interview.

I have done interviews in prisons, in taverns, in hospitals, in churches, and sometimes dark hideaways where the person being interviewed cannot be seen. My brain is so full of personal information, and private testimonies that I sometimes feel like a priest listening to confessions.

As I come to the end of this riveting career, I am somewhat relieved that much of the drama and fabrication that is taking place in today's world will be left behind me. I will no longer be forced to listen, or take sides, or to try to convince people of the truth, when they have been convinced otherwise.

Throughout my career I have reported on planes crashes, terrorist attacks, and school shootings. I have interviewed the mothers of U.S. Navy Seals, and I have visited hospital rooms with soldiers returning from combat with both legs and arms blown off.

I have agonized with grieving individuals after they experience the death of their son or daughter. Many times, I have just sat quietly beside someone for hours, and listened to them wail and morn for the horrendous loss they have experienced. So often they have no one else, and I must become their family.

Maybe I have seen too much. Just watching the American government battle between parties, as they try to destroy the other side's arguments, futures and reputations boggles my mind. They used to pretend that they would all work together if they were elected, but the new people in office refuse to negotiate. There is no longer the reaching across party lines to keep peace; it is their way or the highway. I just cringe as I witness the deterioration of integrity taking place on Capitol Hill, as false accusations and vile hostilities destroy my country.

Hostility is a good word for what is going on, because people today truly seem to despise everything. They hate the President, they don't trust the government, they dislike the police, they recent their employers, they disrespect the military, they detest the media, they insult other nationalities, and they are angry at the church. The confusion is hard to ignore, so most people just live in total disbelief that this could ever happen to America, but it has.

Neighbors have turned on neighbors, friends have turned on friends, and families have turned on their own family members. They argue trying desperately to convince the people around them to believe what they believe. They violently defend their opinion; striving to convince everyone they know that the other side is to blame for the mess the world is in. But no one is ever convinced, and no one ever changes. They just argue until they refuse to ever talk to each other again.

This whole world has gone absolutely crazy, and I have been the eyewitness to too many things. As incredible as my life has been, I am ready to retire and get away from all of the drama, fake-news, and slanderous statements.

My family is grown, I have grandchildren and great-children. It is time for my wife Sarah and me to slow down and have family picnics in the park, and take long leisurely walks along the greenbelt, and watch the river meander through our great city.

Family has always been the most important thing in my life, and now I will have time to attend youth football, baseball, soccer, and basketball games for our grandchildren and great-grandchildren. So many times, I have been forced to miss band concerts, birthday parties, and family get-to-gathers because I was away doing an interview halfway across the world.

My entire life has consisted of deadlines, and article completions, and even if I was in town finalizing something in my home office, I was oftentimes unable to join in the many family events. As a writer, my mind is always working, and I am never finished until the project I am working on is done. It is easier to lock myself in my office, and stay up half the night completing a project, than it is to leave everything, and come back to it later.

After all of my years in journalism, I have come to the conclusion that many politicians create problems just so they can campaign to solve them. There is 1 President, 100 senators, 435 congressmen, and 9 Supreme Court Justices that rule everyone's lives. Those 545 people have control over the rest of the 300 million people that live in the United States, and they decide everything for our country.

With so much division, name-calling, shouting, and threats, the system appears to be broken. Apparently, those 545 people are no longer working for the people who elected them, or the American people on both sides, would not be so outraged.

I can't help but asked myself, "How did we get here?" When I reflect back over my lifetime, I realize it actually started many years ago. Some, of the headlines taken from the national newspapers, social media and the local papers over the past several years explain it all:

On **November 1, 1955 the Vietnam War began**. It was a conflict in Vietnam, Laos and Cambodia. Years later when the vets came home from Vietnam, the Liberal-leftists spit on them and called them baby killers.

On October 6, 1961. **President John F. Kennedy advised all U.S. families to build bomb shelters to protect themselves from fallout** in the event of a nuclear war with the Soviet Union.

On November 22, 1963 President John F. Kennedy was assassinated, as he rode in a motorcade through Dealey Plaza in downtown Dallas, Texas.

Lee Harvey Oswald was arrested for fatally shooting President Kennedy. CNN

Killing or attempting to harm a President was not a federal offense until 1965, two years later.

President Richard Nixon resigns after five men broke into the headquarters of the Democratic National Committee at Watergate. June 17, 1972

Roe v Wade was a landmark 1973 Supreme Court decision that established a woman's right to have an abortion.

Dr. Mildred Jefferson co-founded the national Right to Life organization.

"A Nation that kills its children in the womb, has lost its soul." Mother Teresa

The Fall of Saigon, April 30, 1975; US involvement ended.

Pornography creates serious problems in marriages. CBS

The FDA approved oral contraceptives, and made them available to the general public. The oral contraceptives helped to prevent unwanted pregnancies, but it opened the door for sexual freedom without consequences.

There are more than 20 types of sexually transmitted diseases (STDs).

Mass suicide at Jamestown, Guyana. Peoples Temple founder Jim Jones lead a total of 909 individuals to mass suicide. They drank a powdered drink mix, laced with cyanide. 304 of the members were children. November 18,1978 CNN

The Aryan Nation is an anti-Semitic Neo-Nazi white Supremacists terrorist's organization originally based in Hayden, Idaho, in the seventies. channel 7 news

Ronald Reagan, an American actor defeated incumbent Democrat Jimmy Carter on November 4, 1981, and became the 40th president of the United States.

The Iran-Contra Affair was a secret US arms deal that traded missiles and other arms to free some Americans held hostage by terrorists in Lebanon. August 20, 1985

Space Shuttle Challenger Disaster, January 28, 1986 killing 7 people. Grounding the space shuttle program for almost 3 years.

Federal agents raid the Branch Davidian Compound in Waco, Texas. February 28, 1993 CNN

By the beginning of 1995, 52 school districts had formally adopted **condom availability programs.** ABC

Netflix started in Scotts Valley, California on August 29, 1997.

Google was created September 4, 1998 Menlo Park, California

Monica Lewinsky, the intern involved with President Bill Clinton explains why she signed on for "The Clinton Affair." CBS

President Bill Clinton was impeached, on December 19, 1998, but he apologized and remained in office. CNN

Columbine High School Massacre, April 20, 1999 in Columbine, Colorado leaving 15 dead and 24 seriously injured. CNN

Dan Rather of CBS News got terminated along with several other executives of CBS.

Emmy Award winning journalists Charlie Rose is accused of numerous incidents of sexual misconduct. CBS

Beltway sniper drove a 1990 Chevy Caprice and shot out through the passenger compartment, and the trunk from inside the car, killing several people. CNN

On September 11, 2001 nineteen terrorists who were members of al-Qaeda, an Islamist extreme network, hijacked four commercial airplanes. Two planes flew into the Twin Towers, of the World Trade Center, and the third into the Pentagon. The fourth plane crashed into a field in Pennsylvania, altogether 3,000 people were killed. CNN

43rd President, George W. Bush is best remembered for the September 11, 2001 attack on the World Trade Center.

George W. Bush declares "War on Terrorism."

Operation Enduring Freedom began in Afghanistan. October 7, 2001

After 9/11 George W. Bush established the **Department of Homeland Security.**

Enron an American energy, commodities, and service company based in Houston, Texas declared bankruptcy December 3, 2001 because of accountability fraud and corruption. Approximately 29,000 people lost their jobs. CBS

My Space was created on August 1, 2003.

On April 14, 2003 **The Human Genome Project** was completed.

Facebook was founded by Mark Zuckerberg in his dorm room in July 2003 (it was then called Face Mash)

The International Raelian Movement (Clonaid) might be the world's most science-fictional religion. Their founder claims that he met the aliens who created the human race. CNN

Movies became rated G, PG-13, R, or X

Hip Hop lyrics are the most profane. This shameful music helped transform the language of our youth.

You tube was founded February 14, 2005.

Hurricane Katrina a category 5 hurricane made landfall on Florida and Louisiana, costing $125 billion dollars, and killing more than 1,800 people. It was the costliest national disaster in U.S. history. On August 23, 2005 it flooded New Orleans. The government was very disorganized at completing disaster relief. CBS

Minnesota couple sentenced for making child pornography.

On June 9, 2007 **Apple CEO Steve Jobs released the first iPhone.**

Al Gore speaks out on Climate Change. CBS

Green River Killer is an American serial killer. He murdered at least 49 women in Washington State. CNN

North Korea announced its intention to conduct the first nuclear test. CNN

On April 16, 2007 the Virginia Tech Massacre left 32 dead and was remembered as the 3rd deadliest shooting in U.S. history. CNN

History that is never taught is that the first 23 black senators were all Republicans**.** (Senate.gov.)

George Soros is one of the wealthiest men on the planet, with a personal fortune of at least $7 billion and additional investments of another $11 billion or so. He spends more than $400 million a year to causes ranging from underwriting left-leaning Democratic party candidates to legalizing marijuana or advocating for euthanasia. Soros spent approximately $26 million of his own money in a failed mission to get rid of George Bush. Google

On November 4, 2008 Barack Hussein Obama became America's first black President.

Suspected voter fraud in several counties. Fox News

Globally, it is estimated that there are 20.9 million human trafficking victims. Hannity

May 2, 2011 Death of Osama bin Laden killed by U.S. special operations. CNN

Affordable Care Act nicknamed **Obamacare** was signed into law. CNN

Black Lives Matter movement was developed. Hannity

America is no longer a Christian Nation. Barack Obama 2010

The Islamic State of ISIS is a militant organization that emerged as an offshoot of al-Qaeda.

One of the first widely publicized acts of ISIS violence happened on August 2004 when a few of the group's militants beheaded US journalist James Foley and posted video on You tube. CBS

On February 2015 ISIS released footage of a man being burned alive inside a cage. Fox News

By February 15, 2015 ISIL (ISIS) released a report of the beheading of 21 Coptic Christians on a beach in Libya. CBS

September 11, 2012, there was a coordinated attack against two United States government facilities in Benghazi, Libya by members of the Islamic militant group Ansar al-sharia. Four Americans were brutally killed, including Ambassador Christopher. CNN, CBS, Fox News

Susan Rice tells the National News that the attack on Benghazi was a direct response to a video. CNN, Fox News

Benghazi is a bigger scandal than Watergate. Fox News

Why is **Hillary Clinton blamed** for the **Benghazi attack**? CNN

The Internal Revenue Service targets nonprofit conservatives. Fox News

The Restroom Access Act known as Ally's Law is passed. CNN

The V.A. is in trouble for making patients wait for months to get in to see a doctor. Several veterans die while waiting. Fox News

The Sandy Hook Elementary School Shooting in Newtown, Connecticut was on December 14, 2012. Twenty children were killed, all between the ages of 6 and 7 years old. Six adult staff members were also shot, with 2 injured. Channel 7 news

It is discovered that **Hillary Clinton uses an illegal, unsecured hackable home server**. Fox News

Authorities are investigating the Fast and Furious gunwalking program. Fox News

When a crime is not punished quickly, people feel it is safe to do wrong. Ecclesiastes 8:11 The Bible

Transgender Bathrooms are established so that every student could be allowed to use a bathroom that is consistent with their gender identity. CNN

The Boston Marathon Bombing took place on April 15, 2013. Two pressure cooker bombs killed 3 people and injured 264. Channel 7 News

Bowe Bergdahl charged with desertions and misbehavior. The New York Times

How the Bergdahl story went from victory to controversy for Obama. Time

Extortion 17, Seal Team Six and what really happened on the deadliest day in the history of Naval Special Warfare and the U.S. war in Afghanistan. Hannity

Politicians should wear sponsor jackets like Nascar drivers, then we would know who owns them. Robin Williams

On June 17, 2015 a 21-year-old white supremacist, Dylan Roof murdered 9 African-Americans during a prayer service at the Emanuel African Methodist Episcopal Church, in Charleston, South Carolina. Channel 7 news

On June 26, 2015 the Supreme Court Ruling makes same-sex marriage a right nationwide. CNN

On December 2, 2015, 14 people were killed and 22 others were seriously injured in a terrorist's attack mass shooting and attempted bombing at the Inland Regional Center in San Bernardino, California. Channel 7 News

Former St. Louis police officer acquitted of the murder in the Anthony Lamar Smith case. CNN

Gender neutrality also known as the neutrality movement is established. Fox News

White House trumpets stock market gain under Obama, hits $16,500. CNN

Obamacare make sex change a new reality for 1.4 million Americans. CNBC

The National Law Enforcement Memorial Fund says **64 officers were viciously killed in 2016**. Up more than 50% from the previous year.

Gender neutral toilet facilities will soon be in the public restrooms at Target. Fox News

The Boy Scouts of America may file for bankruptcy because of sex abuse suits. US NEWS

Billionaire financier George Soros gave a fresh $2.5 million to a pro-Hillary Clinton Super Pac in August, part of the $23.4 million. IJR

Donald John Trump is elected the 45th President of the United States. Channel 7 News

The Woman's March was a worldwide march the day after the inauguration of President Trump. CNN

History does not long entrust the care of Freedom to the weak or the tired. Dwight D. Eisenhour 34th President of the United States.

James Comey, the 7th director of the Federal Bureau of Investigation (FBI) was dismissed by President Donald Trump on May 9, 2017. CNN

Dozens of women accuse American film producer Harvey Weinstein of rape, sexual assaults and sexual abuse over the past thirty years. New York Times 2017

Antifa is the moral equivalent of Neo-Nazi. The Washington Post

The Today Show anchor Matt Lauer was fired for inappropriate sexual behavior. CBS News

Most Human Traffickers use psychological means, 'such as' tricks or defrauding, manipulating or threatening their victims. IJR

Update: Kathy Griffin canceled by CNN after a photo of her posing with a severed head of President Donald Trump was publicized. May 31, 2017 CNN

The Dow's gains of 31% during Trump's first year is the best since FDR. Fox News

A gunman opened fire on a crowd of concertgoers at the Harvest Music Festival, killing 58 people and injuring more than 800. Mandalay Bay Resort, October 1, 2017. CNN

Muslim Amazon workers protest lack of prayer breaks. December 17, 2018 Press TV

On October 3, 2018 the Dow Jones Industrial Average's hits its highest closing record at 26, 828.39. Fox News

Democrats behavior at the State of the Union was unbelievable. Florida Politics February 2018

Why are the NFL players taking a knee? Fox News

"If you don't respect our country, then you shouldn't be in this country playing football." Mike Ditka, former American football player, former Head Coach of the Chicago Bears, and the former Head Coach of the New Orleans Saints. Fox News

Half a million credible allegations alleging abuse from leaders in the Catholic Church have been presented. Many of the victims were given a gold cross. The Guardian

May 8, 2018, **Trump declares U.S. is leaving the 'horrible' Iran Nuclear Accord**. Associated Press Chicago

July 2018, Wildfire burns California City. CBS

July 2018, U.S. economy grew at a brisk rate of 4.1 percent from last quarter. USA Today

11 killed in Synagogue Massacre. Suspect charged with 29 counts. CBS

Isis claims attack on France. CNN

Stop letting your T.V. tell you what you hate.

The timeline for the Mueller Investigation into Trump and Russia, is 2017, 2018 and 2019. Fox News

Witches place mass hex on Supreme Court Justice Brett Kavanaugh during New York protest Sunday October 21, 2018 CBS

The opioid category that includes morphine, oxycodone, and hydrocodone was involved in 12,255 deaths in 2017. Fox News

Complaints against Brett Kavanaugh dismissed when he became Supreme Court Justice. CNN

Woman in a vegetation state delivers a baby after being in a coma for years. January 11, 2019 MSN

Phoenix police arrested a 36-year-old nurse at Hacienda Health Care Facility, alleging he sexually assaulted and impregnated a woman at the center. MSN

The numbers are staggering, drug overdose deaths set a record in 2018.

For the men in #MeToo era, they say Mike Pence' rule is dumb, lazy and the easy way out. Lifezette

Crossing attempts at the US Southwest border tripled in March from one year ago. Washington Post 2018

Lady Gaga slams Vice President Mike Pence for his Christian values for tolerating wife's work at a Christian school. CBS

On line dating site seen by 7,000 viewers daily. 2019

Nearly 1 in 3 students report being bullied during the school year. NCES National Center for Education Statistics

13-year-old boy commits suicide after bullies 'encouraged him to kill himself.' Faves USA

Approximately 34% of students report experience cyberbullying during their lifetime. Faves USA

Government shutdown "Is there a crisis on the Mexican border?" January 2019 CNN

Democrats vacation in Puerto Rico with 109 lobbyists during the government shutdown, January 2019. Fox News

Miley Cyrus claims, "Satan Is a Nice Guy. He is just misunderstood." IJR

"I can almost understand President Trump's decision to ground Nancy Pelosi and her traveling delegates during the government shutdown. CNN

President Donald Trump thanks Robert Mueller for disputing the Cohen report. Fox News

Trump prepares to offer DACA protection for the border wall and to re-open the government. USA Today

CNN claims there were only around 1,000 people attending the 46th annual 2019 March for Life, anti-abortion rally in Washington D.C. Live coverage shows that there were actually tens of thousands of marchers in attendance. CNN

The next generation of voters are more liberal, and more inclusive, and believe in government. Washington Post 2019

Baby born to transgender man, could be the first person born without a legal mother. UK World News, News Britain

Nancy Pelosi told President Trump he could not deliver the State of the Union address from the House chambers during the government shutdown. CNN, New York Times, and CBS News

The Department of Homeland Security estimates that immigration (legal or illegal) comprise 20 per cent of the inmates in prisons and jails. IJR

Toxic Masculinity is under attack. Toxic Masculinity is a soldier keeping you safe since 1776.

New York Senate Passes Bill Legalizing Abortion up to Birth. Life News

New York celebrates legalizing abortion until birth by lighting One World Trade Center the color pink. Fox News

Prominent Catholics demand New York governor Andrew Cuomo be excommunicated from the Catholic Church over the new abortion law. CNN

Governor Cuomo of New York signed a landmark legislation protecting LGBTQ rights. Bans transgender discrimination making it a hate crime under New York law. Pressroom, Live report

President Donald Trump said, "I **signed a letter to congress** to make it clear that if they send any legislation to my desk that weakens the protection of human life, I will issue a veto." "Every child is a sacred gift from God." Every life is worth protecting. When we look into the eyes of a newborn child, we see the beauty and the human soul and the majesty of God's creation. We know that every life has meaning and that every life is worth protecting."

2019 Technology Replacing Business Phones and Landlines.

Winter of 2018-2019, 20 degrees colder than normal. CNN

One dead and twelve hospitalized in a mass overdose in Chico, California. Channel 7 News

Democrats say, "The red MEGA Donald Trump hat is the new white KKK hood." The Patriot Post

California restaurant owner flat-out refuses to serve customers wearing Mega Trump hats. Fox News

Outbreak of measles in Oregon. 2019 Channel 7 News

Text and Drive: Violation of the law is a misdemeanor punishable by a fine of $25 for the first offense, $50 for the second offense, and $75 for the third offense. (varies in every state)

In 2018, several states considered bills that would legalize adult-use marijuana. Governing News

Who are the Black Israelites? The DC group calls itself "House of Israel." The Blaze

Border patrol agent stated, "Let me say it this way, I have seen 6 different presidents in the time that I have been with the Border Patrol, but the **illegal immigrant situation is the worse than I have ever seen it." January 2019** (Live report)

Heart-beat bill... If we can see a heart-beat, it is a person. OB-GYN who delivered over 2,500 babies. Western Journal

You can't spank your child, but you can kill it a few minutes before it is born. Glenn Beck

Today it is the unborn child; tomorrow it is likely to be the elderly or those who have an incurable illness. Who knows but later it may be anyone who has political or moral values that do not fit into the distorted New Order? Dr. Mildred Jefferson

The abortion bill isn't about 'Women's Health', It's about killing babies. Fox News

Over population and the build-up of human generated greenhouse gases is the real cause of climate change. It's killing all of us. The Center for Biological Diversity

Planned parenthood kept aborted babies alive to harvest its heart and brain. Washington Times

Ideas on immigrants and being an American in 1907: In the first place we should insist that if the immigrants who comes here in good faith becomes an American, and assimilates himself to us, he shall be treated on an exact equality with everyone else, for it is an outrage to discriminate against any such man because of creed, or birthplace, or origin. But this is predicated upon the person's becoming in every facet an American, and nothing but an American… There can be no divided allegiance here. Any man who says he is an American, but something else also, isn't an American at all. We have room for but one flag, the American flag…We have room for but one language here**,** and that is the English language…And we have room for but one sole loyalty and that is a loyalty to the American people. Theodore Roosevelt 1907

At least 79 Mexican people were killed after an explosion, while stealing gasoline from a Mexican pipeline. Channel 7 News

No domestic abuser should have more rights than the victim. Hannity

Child porn ring leader killed in prison, beaten by other inmates. Rare

Mike Pence claims that Nancy Pelosi's refusal to negotiate tells Americans everything they need to know about Democrats. They plan their speeches before President Trump even gives his speech. Fox News

New bill would allow public schools to offer Bible studies as an elective. The Blaze

In every state it is illegal to drive with the BAC of .08 or higher. Yet, there is a person killed in a drunk driving crash every 48 minutes in the United States.

Covington student Nicholas Sandmann and family have hired an attorney to sue media for libel. NBC

Authorities warn about sex trafficking luring teens via gaming apps, 7 arrested. Fox News

Psychology Today says video games leave kids revved up, stressed out, and primed for a meltdown. Playing violent video games mimic the kinds of sensory assaults humans are programmed to associate with danger. Psychology Today

Kamala Harris launches 2020 bid for the Whitehouse with promise of Free college, Free Medical for all, and no plan for funding anything. IJR Red

Booker T. Washington "A lie doesn't become truth, wrong doesn't become right, and evil doesn't become good, just because it's accepted by the majority."

Border patrol wives invite Nancy Pelosi to visit the border. Fox News

Attorney for Nick Sandmann from the Covington Catholic School; says the media, and celebrities who attacked students need to be punished and pay a huge price. Washington Post

Pentagon sending 3,750 more troops to the Mexican Border. Channel 7 News

After the government was reopened, Chuck Schumer stated, "Hopefully now the President has learned his lesson." The Patriot Post (Live report)

When the President reopened the government, Nancy Pelosi declared that she had changed her mind, "A wall is not who we are as a nation." MRCTV

President Donald Trump's job approval up 7 points after the shutdown. Gallup

Deadly polar vortex blasts Midwest. January 2019 Channel 7 News

Mumps have been detected in Utah. Channel 7 News

New bill aims to charge mothers for assault if babies are addicted to drugs when they are born. Rare Us

Democrats to strike 'So help me God' from oath. Fox News

Ex-Trump advisor, Roger Stone was arrested before dawn by 29 federal agents, dressed in full tactical gear, and arriving in 17 squad cars at his home in Fort Lauderdale, Florida. He was arrested as part of the Mueller probe investigation. Police came with lights flashing, weapons drawn, and arrived at the house at 6:00 a.m., before daylight. People are questioning how the **CNN reporters were notified in advance, so that they could be there for the exclusive footage of the arrest. CNN also knew in advance that it was not a dangerous situation because they stood within 25 feet of Roger Stone and his wife as they filmed.** Hannity

There was more firepower at Roger Stone's house than there was on the roof of the U.S. Consulate in Benghazi. The Patriot Post

"Speak up for those who cannot speak for themselves; ensure justice for those being crushed." Proverbs 31:8 The Bible

Wrongful death suit filed for Alabama baby aborted against father's wishes. Lifezette

A young man is suing his parents for giving birth to him 'without' his consent, and he may win. Fox News

"There is room in America and brotherhood for all who will support our instructions, and aid in our development. But those who come to disturb our peace, and to dethrone our lives are aliens and enemies forever." MEME

Teachers arrested for locking autistic students in a dark bathroom. The daily beast

People who support killing unborn children have no moral authority to lecture the nation on their opinion that building a wall is immoral. The Blaze

South Carolina lawmakers propose criminalizing abortion. The BL

People in the United States have had guns in their homes for over 200 years. And mass shootings have only become a problem in the last 30 years. If you look there is a huge correlation between the use of gun shootings, and the decline of disciplining your children.

"We do have a generation that I think we have raised with a great deal of entitlement...We've got to stop rewarding bad behavior in America. When people don't work and produce, then they need to get kicked to the curb. Get a job!" Dr. Phil MRC TV

Border Patrol completes largest Fentanyl bust in U.S. History. Seizing over 250 pounds of lethal drugs. Enough to kill over 50 million people. Fox News

Washington state officials declare a state of emergency with an outbreak of 42 cases of measles. Fox News

Report: Tijuana becomes the 'deadliest city in the world.' Homicides are up 700% since 2012. Hannity

"And gradually though no one remembered exactly how it happened, the unthinkable becomes tolerable, and then acceptable, and then legal, and then applaudable." (Joni Eareckson Tada)

Freedom is never more than one generation away from extinction. (Ronald Reagan)

"When you can't find Russian collusion on President Trump…You indict everybody around him on process crimes that have nothing to do with Russia or Trump." Hannity

Payrolls surge by 304,000, smashing estimates despite government shutdown. **Best January in 30 years.** CNBC

Biased media praises Nancy Pelosi as SOTU 'Genius.' MSNBC Chris Mathews

"Nancy Pelosi stole the show. It was the show behind the show, nodding her head no when President Trump declared that the State of the Union is strong." Washington Post

Hillary Clinton praises the genius Nancy Pelosi. Clinton said, "Yet again, it often takes a woman to get the job done." Fox News

Drag Queen who goes by the name of 'Annie Christ' reads to kids at the public library!" The Blaze, CBN News

LGBTQ activist S. Bear Bergman noted a similar sentiment in his 2015 Huffington Post piece, "I have come to Indoctrinate your children into the LGBT agenda. (I'm not a bit sorry) "Groom the next generation!" "Stop the Hate, Drag is great!" The Huffington Post

2018: The year it was easier for President Trump to strike a deal with a communist dictator than it was with the Democratic party. The Patriotic Post

A Nation divided against itself cannot stand. Abraham Lincoln

"When a Nation turns its back on God. The end is near." Franklin Graham

"I hope people will just turn their TV's off and not watch the President's State of the Union." Maxine Waters CNN News

Numerous states introduce Bible Literary classes as electives. The Blaze

US becomes UK's top oil suppliers for first time since Suez. USA Today

The League of Nazi Socialist women who supported Hitler's dream of socialist paradise, always went to the events dressed in white. The Blaze

At the State of the Union address, the majority of the Democrat women all dressed in white. All major Network Broadcast stations

Nancy Pelosi and her 'white pant suit crew' take heat for sitting stone-faced through much of President Trump's SOTU. LIFEZETTE

Ted Cruz denounces the Democrats for disrespecting the office of the President during the State of the Union address. Lifezette. Com

CNN Instant Poll shortly after the state of the union address says 76% of Americans approved of President Trumps message. CNN

Trump's pro-life State of the Union comments were nothing short of historic. Fox News

Since 1973 there has been 60 million babies aborted in America.

Sean Hannity said, "The State of the Union shows that Trump is for 'We the people' and Democrats are for hating Trump." Fox News

American Jews thank President Trump in a full-page New York Times ad after the State of the Union Address. Fox News

"He who walks in integrity walks securely." Proverbs 10:9 The Bible

President Donald Trump was given the Ellis Island Award for 'Patriotism, tolerance, brotherhood and diversity alongside Muhammed Ali and Rosa Parks in 1986. app.news.com

President Trump's State of the Union is a symphony of pure genius! This was one of the best SOTU addresses that there has ever been. Rush Limbaugh

"Every once in a while, a speech is so effective and powerful it changes the trajectory of history." Newt Gingrich Fox News

"In America we don't worship government, we worship God." President Donald Trump

Church opens doors to 225 homeless people, letting them sleep inside every night. Winter 2019 Fox News

President Trump says he wants to boost US legal immigration because unemployment is so low. State of the Union Address

The question is; will they decide at some point that they love this country more than they hate this President? Will they be willing to actually focus on what they were elected to do? Fox News

"Victory is not for our winning party...victory is for winning for our country." President Trump, State of the Union

"And let us reaffirm a fundamental truth: All children born and unborn are made in the holy image of God." President Donald Trump, State of the Union

Patriots Around USA "In case you haven't figured it out yet-I'm not your typical Republican...I fight back." President Donald J. Trump

Liz Cheney calls out the Democrat women for applauding themselves, but not Trumps mention on US values at SOTU. IJR RED

The pro-abortion left has morphed into a death cult, under the guise of protecting women's health. IJR

"They shed innocent blood, the blood of their sons and daughters, whom they sacrificed to the idols of Canaan, and the land was desecrated by their blood." Psalm 106:38 The Bible

Parents are hosting chicken pox parties so their kids can get it over with, but pediatricians say the practice is a gamble. Fox News

New Jersey has officially become the second state in the Nation to require public schools to teach LGBT history. Faves USA

Southern Baptist leaders condemn decades of sexual abuse within their own churches. Washington Post

"I am asking the congress to pass legislation to prohibit Late-Term abortion of children who can feel pain in the mother's womb." President Donald Trump, State of the Union

"Nancy Pelosi you are a hypocrite, and a political operative. Your mantra…Destroy the President of the United States. Ms. Pelosi does not have your interest at heart. She is an obstructionist and an embarrassment**."** Judge Judy Pirro Fox News

State of the Union Poll: Approval of speech, Republicans 97%, Democrats 30%, and Independents 82%. **February 7, 2019** Fox News

"We were born free and we will stay free. America will never be a socialist country." President Donald Trump, State of the Union

Socialism victims warn the American people: "Bernie Sanders is your enemy. Don't fall for it, people on socialism are starving and they are eating out of trash cans." CNS NEWS

Kellyanne Conway says she was physically assaulted, at a restaurant by a Trump hater. CNN

President Trumps SOTU was well received by most viewers but not by Democrats. Fox News

February 8, 2019 As Border Wall funding divides Washington, new multimillion-dollar barrier will soon break ground in Texas. Fox News

The Monitor Update: 1,000 pounds of methamphetamine was seized at Pharr Port entry today. Fox News

Texas rancher offers his land for border wall. He said, "Mr. President you're right on the money; get this done!" Lifezette

"You can't get rich in politics unless you're a crook." Harry S. Truman

Embattled Governor of Virginia, Ralph Northern vowed to remain in office even after pictures of him in Black-face appeared. He stated, "There is no better person to help heal the state from the multitude of scandals, than me; because I'm a doctor." Fox News

"We're not joking, Ocasio-Cortez wants to upgrade or replace every single building in the US." Western Journal

Republicans introduce House version of bill banning infanticide after failed abortions. Fox News

President Trump follows through on his promise to donate his entire salary to Better America. IJR Red

Texas police form a wall of vehicles to aid border patrol to stop caravan migrants near Eagle Pass, Texas. Fox News

California governor Gavin Newsom plans to order the National guard troops back from the border with Mexico to rebuff President Donald Trump. So, he is trying to overpower the President now. What is really going on in our country? Newsbreak and Fox News

Los Angeles, California is now a sanctuary city. CNN

Breaking News: 'The Rock' just laid the smackdown on Nancy Pelosi to step aside and let President Trump do his job! Fox News

FEC refuses to probe alleged $84 million Clinton campaign laundering. The Federalist.com, Fox New

Trump wants a Photo ID in every state in order to vote. Fox News

Senator Ted Cruz and Rep. Frances Rooney introduce amendment to set term limits on congress. The Blaze

60 years ago, Venezuela was ranked 4th on the world economic Freedom Index. Today, they are ranked 174th and their citizens are dying from starvation. In only 10 years Venezuela was destroyed by "Democratic Socialism." Hannity

I can't side with any politician who has been in office since 1981, and blames a new President for America's problem. IJR

Washington shocked at Trump's approval rate is 52% Rush Limbaugh February 11, 2019

Rep. Alexandria Ocasio-Cortez says migrants crossing the Border are more American than any person who seeks to keep them out. MSN

Green New Deal: Ocasio-Cortez aims to make air travel obsolete. "It may take as long as ten years, because we aren't sure if we can get rid of the cow gas and airplanes that fast." Lifezette

President Trump calls Ocasio-Cortez Green New Deal a 'High School term paper that got a low mark." It would shut down air travel. How do you take a train to England? Live report

Nancy Pelosi gets rock star treatment at Clive Davis gala in Beverly Hills, California. CBS News

Nancy Pelosi recreates smug SOTU clap, mocking Trump with Katy Perry at Grammys party. CNN

After the Abortion victory, Democrats push for Physicians assisted suicide. Western Journal

Human Trafficking arrest since 2010: 3,213 in 2017, and **5,987 in 2018.** IJR

Henry Kissinger, the former Secretary of State gives a new understanding of President Donald Trump. "Donald Trump is a phenomenon that foreign countries haven't seen before. The man is doing changes like never before and does all of it for the sake of this nation's people. After eight years of tyranny, we finally see a difference. Kissinger puts it bluntly: Trump puts America and its people first. People need to open their eyes!"

Democrats won't fund a Border Wall to keep illegals out...but they expect you to fund sanctuary cities to keep them in. Hannity

Border-Security advocates form a 'human wall' along US-Mexico border. Fox News

159 confirmed cases of measles. Channel 7 News

A movement is spreading: Teens are reportedly seeking vaccinations without parental consent. The Blaze

The Fox News Channel is the top cable network for the 17th year.

"The weak grow strong by effrontery. The strong grow weak through inhibition." Henry Kissinger

"One of the best comments I saw online was from someone in the Yahoo News comments section, who said President Donald Trump reminded him of a doctor with no bedside manner. He tells you that you need to lose 100 pounds and stop smoking. You're offended, you're angry, and you come up with 10 reasons why he's crazy…and then you finally realize that he's the only one telling you the truth. Mike Huckabee

Michelle Obama's appearance at the Grammys splits audience. Some say they will never watch the Grammys again. Lifezette

"We don't have anything: Senate Intel Chairman says panel has no proof of collusion between Trump and Russia." IJR

A Texas man bought a Texas-sized message billboard about Donald Trump and the media. It said, "ABC News I grew up with you. We are through. The media didn't elect Donald Trump. I did!" Rare US

IIhan Omars AIPAC sparks condemnation from both parties after she accused a prominent lobbying group of paying members of congress to support Israel. Fox News

Obamas ambassador to Israel demands Democrats call out IIhan Omar's anti-Semitism February 2019 Fox News

In Islam you have to die for Allah. The God I worship died for me. Franklin Graham

Covington High School students cleared of any wrongdoing after independent investigation. Fox News

Angel families return to Nancy Pelosi's office to share their stories and to request a border wall. They had an appointment, but once again Nancy Pelosi would not allow them in. Fox News

Democrats Omar and Tlaib introduced an "order of Tabbouleh" and demanded it be brought into congress as a fundamental to their roots and culture. February 13, 2019 Lifezette

White couple who identifies as black say their children will be born black. CSBSN

"Death to America" Iran lashes out on 40th Anniversary of Revolution." Conservative review

Oklahoma Senator introduces bill to criminalize late-term abortions as first-degree murder. Fox News

Hannity Gallup poll: 69% of Americans optimistic on economy, 50% feel better off, Highest since 1998.

Ted Cruz wants to pass 'El Chapo Act' to make notorious drug lord pay for border wall. CBS

New Mexico governor removes National Guard from border while slamming Trump. Lifezette

Democrat Omar wants Homeland Security defunded, says Trump's 'hateful wall' should not be built. Lifezette

Just revealed: Muslim Democrat Rep Rashida Tlaib wrote for Louis Farrakhan's publication. The Blaze

Donald Trump calls on freshman Democrat IIhan Omar to 'resign from Congress' over her Israel comments. President Trump condemned lame apology.

Pence echoes Trump on Rep. Omar's Anti-Semitic statements. Calls for her to 'Face the consequences.' Fox News

Cuomo slams Ocasio-Cortez, as Amazon dumps New York headquarters and its promised 25,000 jobs. Fox News

American Joe once again states that the media is lying! They are still bringing in money for a go fund me campaign to help President Trump build the wall. Lifezette

Networks: 2,202 minutes on Russia scandal, zero for no collusion report. We spent 40 million dollars to find out that Trump was simply elected by American patriots. Sarah Palin and Sean Hannity

Rasmussen Poll: Trump's Presidency approval rating reaches near two-year high. Highest point since shortly after Inauguration MRCTV

Progressive Education hard at work. Student's carry a sign that said: Trump is the Symptom. Capitalism is the Disease and Socialism is the cure. Freedom Project

A record number of Americans are 90 days behind on their car payments. CNBC

"We've been conditioned to think that only politicians can solve our problems. But at some point, maybe we will wake up and recognize that it was politicians who created our problems." Ben Carson

Kids pour boiling water on each other as part of "Hot Water Challenge." Western Journal

The border wall would devastate drug and sex trafficking businesses. Sean Hannity

The FBI scrambled to respond to Hillary Clinton lawyer amid Weiner laptop review… newly released emails shown. Fox News

Man stabs pregnant girlfriend, killing baby but won't be charged for murder because of New York abortion law. The Political

Sherriff's warn ICE (US Immigration and Customs Enforcement) could be forced to release 8,300 criminal aliens. Daily Caller

Teens are playing a reckless new challenge game. They are sneaking out of their house and hiding from their parents for several days. Channel 2 news

Hating Trump is more important to Dems than the **safety** of Americans. Hannity

Millennials are having large 'Solo gamy' ceremonies instead of real weddings, they having all of the festivities and marry themselves. The parents don't approve of solo gamy weddings. The person decides after several failed relationships, just to have a large wedding and marry themselves. Lifezette

Taxes didn't go up, people just paid less all year**.** The Patriot Post

Dem leaders would have funded the wall months ago if it was their child who was killed. Angel Dad

American financial optimism reaches a 16-year-high. IJR

The United Nations wants a One-World government in less than 12 years. Lifezette

Christian group to combat 'No Abortion Law' with live ultrasounds played in times Square. Westernjournal.com

Ocasio-Cortez faces heat for Amazon cancelling NYC plan. Mike Huckabee, Fox News

Baby Boomers needed 306 hours of minimum wage work to pay a 4-year public college debt. Millennials needed 4,459 hours. The National Center for Education Statistics

Border Patrol apprehends huge group of 325 illegal immigrants at once. Many are unaccompanied juveniles. Western Journal

Gender Open parenting; the parents will not restrict their child's gender so they call their child a 'theyby' until they are old enough to decide what sex they want to be. Glenn Beck (Live Report with child's mother)

Many colleges have started Diversity and Inclusion training. Diversity is the range of human differences, including but not limited to race, ethnicity, gender, gender identity, sexual orientation, age, social class, physical ability, religions or ethical value system, national origin and potential beliefs. Five diversity and inclusion trends we can expect to see in 2019: Male executive apologies, #MeToo after effects, diverse leadership, inclusive products, and celebrities speaking out.

State of Union speech poll released, February 9, 2019: Approve of speech, Republicans 97%, Democrats 30%, and Independents 82%.

"We are comedians and I refuse to use my show to do serious dialog. Once a comedian starts that it is dangerous because we are making ourselves out to be too important; as if our personal opinion on critical issues matter. As comedians we should never mix the world's situations with the jokes and humor that we provide. When a comedian starts voicing his opinion on world issues, he has overstepped his bounds, and he has lost his purpose." Jonny Carson

Jimmy Kimmel and Jimmy Fallon raked over the coals for Blackface silence! TMN Today

Frustration grows as a migrant caravan is stuck in a Mexican shelter in Piedras Negras, across from Eagle Pass, Texas with 1,600 Central American migrants. Lifezette

Elizabeth Warren, one of the Democratic candidates for President declares Trump could be jailed by the time the 2020 presidential elections roll around. CBS News

We are only one election away from losing the constitution. Glenn Beck

Bill Gates tears into Alexandria Ocasio-Cortez when it comes to tax policy missing the picture. IJR

Ocasio-Cortez wants you to take a train, but she spent 7 times more on plane travel than on Amtrak. Western Journal

Bloomingdales apologizes for selling 'Fake News' T-shirts. Washington Post

Florida school hires combat vets with semiautomatic rifles to protect students from active shooters. The Blaze

And the man God chose was neither a politician nor a priest. Instead, God chose Nehemiah. "And the first step of rebuilding the nation was the building of a great wall, God instructed Nehemiah to build a wall around Jerusalem to protect its citizens from enemy attack. Nehemiah, the Bible

Trump unhappy with budget proposal, yet doesn't foresee another government shut-down. Lifezette

700,000 US children are homeless. "When will we put Americans first?" IJR

Infant who survived abortion screamed for an hour while left alone to die. Fox News

Trump officially calls for Rep. IIhan Omar to leave congress after anti-Semitic, "Hook-nosed" tweets. Western Journal

FBI's Andrew McCabe uses book and TV to defend the indefensible. Andrew McCabe admits he tried to organize a 25th Amendment coup to oust President Trump. Western Journal

America can survive without athletes, but it can't survive without the American soldier. Lifezette

Senate confirms Trumps attorney general who opposes Roe v Wade. Fox News

Chicago ranked most corrupt city in the United States. Hannity report

Rep. IIhan Omar snaps at CNN reporter asking questions she didn't like. Western Journal

Trump polls at 52 per cent. Best approval rate in 23 months. (February 14, 2019 Hannity)

Judge orders state of California to pay $399K to pro-life pregnancy centers. The Blaze

Jewish diplomat decided he had enough of IIhan Omar's hate remarks during a special hearing, and he stopped answering her. Fox News live report

William Barr secures votes to be confirmed by senate for attorney general. Fox News.

February 15, 2019, President Donald Trump announces we will sign emergency declaration for border wall. Fox News

DOJ held meeting on how to oust President Trump. Fox News

New polls show that overwhelming population oppose to late term abortion. Lifezette

Apple removes Christian ministry apps. following complaints by LGBT activists. The Blaze

Students-activist groups nationwide issued demands to their Universities seeking everything from mandatory sensitivity and racial-bias training to development of safe spaces on campuses for people of color.

Linda Sarsour, an American political activist, best known for her hatred for Israel says she wants Muslims to form 'Jihad' against Trump and not to assimilate. She was born in 1980 in New York City. She was the co-chair of the 2017 Women's March**.** Live report

Boy Scouts of America are now welcoming girls. Lifezette

Alexandria Ocasio-Cortez faces questions after her boyfriend gets congressional email account. Her boyfriend's name is found on staff roster, and reports show that her chief of staff cut checks to her boyfriend using a PAC. Western Journal

Nancy Pelosi says a Democratic President could declare gun violence a National Emergency. Fox News

Obama border patrol chief leads calls for the border wall at Angel family's event: 'Enough is Enough' speaks out for President Trump's border security. Fox News

Jussie Smollett faces felony charges for allegedly filing a fake hate crime police report. He staged a raciest anti-gay attack with his 'pretend' attackers yelling "This is Mega Country." Fox News

"You cannot legislate the poor into freedom by legislating the wealthy out of freedom. What one person receives without working for, another person must work to pay. The government cannot give to anybody without first taking from somebody else. When half of the people get the idea that they do not have to work because the other half is going to take care of them. The working half will soon get the idea that it does no good to work, because somebody else is going to get what they have worked for. That my dear friends, is about the end of any nation. You cannot multiply wealth by dividing it." Dr. Adrian Rogers 1931

"America will never be destroyed from the outside. If we falter and lose our freedoms, it will be because we destroyed ourselves!" President Abraham Lincoln

Reagan-We have a border crisis…

Bush Sr.-We have a border crisis…

Clinton-We have a border crisis…

Bush Jr.-We have a border crisis…

Obama-We have a border crisis…

Trump-We have a border crisis "Let's build a wall and solve the border crisis."

Libs, "Trump manufactured the border crisis."

TRUMP ON BORDER SECURITY: "Just so you know… We will build the wall!" quote from President Donald Trump

"It's anyone's guess what happens next. Democrats shoot down Trumps plans." USA Today, February 2019

New study shows people like dogs more than humans. IHEARTDOGS.COM

The news used to tell you that something happened, and then you had to decide what you thought about it. Now, the news tells you how to think about something, and you have to decide if it EVEN happened. Walter Cronkite

Whoever speaks the truth gives honest evidence, but a false witness utters deceit. Proverbs 12:17

"We will take America without firing a shot...We will Burry You! We can't expect the American people to jump from Capitalism to Communism, but we can assist your elected leaders in giving them small doses of Socialism, until they awaken one day to find that they have communism. We do not have to invade the United States; we will destroy it from within!" **Nikita Khrushchev...1956**

Freedom is never more than one generation away from extinction. We didn't pass it to our children in the bloodstream. It must be fought for, protected, and handed on for them to do the same, or one day we will spend our sunset years telling our children and our children's children what it was once like in the United States when men were free. Ronald Reagan

Put on the full armor of God, so that when the day of evil comes you may be able to stand your ground. (Ephesians 6:11-13 NIV Bible)

***

The Lord has given me a beautiful home, a strong church family, and a wonderful community of friends to laugh with, talk with and just be grateful to have around. I have always appreciated the security of my hometown, but with all of the changes that have taken place throughout my lifetime, I think I appreciate it even more, than I ever did before.

Because of all the things that I have seen and experienced throughout the years I will be glad to relax, in the comfort of my own home, with my own family, in my own community, and just sip a cup of hot coffee and enjoy watching the sunset from my back deck.

It is almost time for Sarah and me to pack up our fifth wheel, and travel, and leave all of the hate and nonsense of the media behind us. There are museums, state campgrounds, NASCAR races, amusement parks, monuments, and flea-markets still left to be crossed off of our bucket list.

The kids got me a new fishing pole for Christmas last year, and the time has come to try it out, and go fishing in some of Idaho's beautiful lakes and streams. I'll be glad to just sit by a campfire, drink hot chocolate and roast marshmallows.

Retirement means I will no longer have to listen to all of the arguing, and animosity that is continually taking place in the political rallies, news conferences, and the television news reports.

Many times, in my life I have been forced to interview, reflect and report about things that sadden, repulse or sometimes even confuse me. After all of these years, maybe it is finally time for me to escape from the never-ending corruption, hate, transformations, and sadness that seem to dominate the news. The news is not about news anymore. It's about protecting some people, and destroying others.

Today is February 22, 2019, the day of my retirement party. From this day on, I will no longer have to worry about, who is right or who is wrong.

After sixty remarkable years my journalism career is complete. I will never have to do another interview, or eyewitness report again. It is time to let someone else try to resolve the world's problems.

Beginning tomorrow, I will sit back, and let the rest of the world write the ending to this story.

Sincerely,

D. L. Jacobson

At the end of your life, you will never regret not having passed one more test, or winning one more verdict, or not closing one more deal. You will only regret times not spent with a spouse, a friend, a child or a parent.

Barbara Bush

Made in the USA
Middletown, DE
06 November 2021